WIFED BY A BOSS 2

MS. KEENA

D1522916

TEXT UCP TO 22828 TO SUBSCRIBE TO OUR
MAILING LIST
If you would like to join our team, submit the first 3-4
chapters of your completed manuscript to
Submissions@UrbanChapterspublications.com

ACKNOWLEDGMENTS

Thank you, thank you, thank you to everyone that took the time out to purchase this book and all my other books. You guys don't know how nerve wracking it was worrying if you guys would like it.

To my heartbeats, you are a reflection of me, so it's only right that I show you that anything can be accomplished with motivation. I hope that I am the inspiration that you seek when times get tough.

To my love, my best friend, and my biggest supporter, Charles, it only gets better. All the trials and tribulations will finally pay off as long as we stay strong together.

To my readers, thank you for your continued support. You guys gave me the push I needed with the numerous inboxes, comments, and reviews.

To my family, both near and far, thank you for the calls, texts, and support of ordering books. It's because of your support through word of mouth and sharing posts on Facebook that these books have a success.

Follow me:
Twitter: @Theauthorkeena
Instagram: theauthorkeena
Facebook: Sakina Thomas & Author Keena
Facebook Author Page: Author Keena
Reading Group: Sakina Sensational Readers

PREVIOUSLY...

Budah

This couldn't be fucking happening. My lady, brother, and sis-in-law were all in the same fucking hospital at one time. I was sitting there with Miya, Robi, and Blessing waiting on news about everyone. As I was waiting, Tez walked in. We dapped it up and walked over to a corner.

"What's good?" I asked.

"Yo, Ameka was fighting Asha, and from what I'm hearing, her mother was in on it too. Asha's homegirl right there was trying to fight them off with her, so you might want to go and say something to her," Tez said.

"What the fuck? I know her and her mother don't get down like that, but to set her up to get jumped is fucked up. Find Asha's mother, Ameka, and anyone else that has something to do with it. I know them niggas in the hood recorded that shit too. I want all phones that have the videos, and I mean every one of them. When you get them all together, take all of them to the warehouse by the water and tie them all up," I responded.

I walked over the chick that was sitting by the soda machine. I saw that Blaze, Snow, and Reese had walked in, so I guess they heard the news about Kamari.

"Yo, you Asha's friend?" I asked.

"Yeah, I'm Monica," she replied.

"Well, come over here and sit with the family. I appreciate you helping Asha," I replied.

"It's nothing. Asha and I were kicking ass back in middle school, so it's only right I knock a couple bitches out for GP," she replied.

As we were walking over to everyone, the doctor came out. "The family of Asha Gray?"

"Right here!" Aunt Robi called out.

"Hello I'm Dr. Channing. Ms. Gray sustained an injury to the back of her head and to her back. I believe that it was a bat or something in that shape. When she was hit in the back, one of her ribs were cracked, so she will feel pain from that once the meds wear off. She doesn't have a concussion, but if she experiences blurriness, sensitivity to sunlight, or anything like that, bring her back. She also has about ten stitches in her head. She will have to come back to have those removed or see her family doctor."

"Thank you. When can we see her?" Aunt Robi asked.

"I can take two back right now," he responded.

"Go 'head back, Robi. I'll be back after I talk to the fellas," I responded.

Once she went back with Monica, I went outside to the parking garage where all the bosses were waiting on me.

"What's up, Budah?" one of the asked.

"Today is the day that the bloodshed will begin for the next seven days. I almost lost the lives of my loved ones because motherfuckers think that it's a game. I know for a fucking fact that we have at least three people that are CIs to the cops, and they will be dealt with the way I see fit. I gave everyone of y'all a chance to clean your house, and it fell on deaf ears. Blaze and Tez will give each one of you an assignment that will be carried out. Motherfuckers will feel my wrath by the time that I am finished, and it won't stop until I'm satisfied. Right now, I must go back and check on my family. Dismissed," I stated

When I walked back into the hospital, I went back to check on Asha. Her clothes were bloody, and her hair was matted from the blood. When she saw me, it was a mixture of tears and anger.

"You alright, ma?" I asked, kissing her forehead.

"Yeah, can we get out of here?" she asked.

"I can have Robi take you home, but I can't leave," I stated.

"Why not?" she asked.

"Mari and Justice are here," I announced.

"What do you mean they are here!" she shouted.

"They were shot at. I'm waiting to hear what is going on with them. I haven't heard anything from the doctors yet," I replied.

"Okay, well, let's go find out what's going on with them. What I look like going home when they are still here?" she responded. "Monica, you're still here? I thought you would've left," she said.

"Nah, I'm right here. I called my brother to go and pick up my daughter," Monica replied.

I just knew that she was going to curse my ass out, and I might not even be in the clear because she was too calm with the information she just learned. The entire time that she was talking to Monica, she was cutting her eyes at me and rolling them. I felt helpless that my baby brother was in the hospital, and I couldn't get any information from no one.

When we made it to the emergency waiting room, Asha went into complete bitch mode.

"Excuse me! Can someone tell me what the fuck is going in with my sister and my brother-in-law? We have been waiting too fucking long, and no one has said shit yet!" she shouted.

"Ma'am, I'm going to need you to calm down," the nurse said.

"Oh, I am calm. Now you can get someone out here, or I will be walking through those doors and getting answers myself," she stated.

While she was going off, I couldn't even be mad at her, because she was right. I called my OG and gave him the latest, and he told me that he and his brothers would be here in a couple of hours.

I had been cool long enough. It was now time for me to start wrecking shit again. Niggas didn't know that I could give a fuck about having mothers, sisters, and babies, or anyone else in all black, selling dinners to pay for a fucking funeral. They wanted a war. Well, now they had one. I hoped they were ready because I stayed ready. Say hello to the bad guy!

ASHA

I can't believe that we were sitting here waiting to get some sort of news about Justice and Kamari. I had never seen any signs of pain in Kairo's face, so imagine my expression when he was telling me that both Justice and Mari were here. We were all sitting here with a shocked and worried look on our faces, when none other than Kendra walked in with her dramatic antics. All that falling out and crying for nothing, but she was just threatening the lives of both them other day.

"I need someone to give me some answers," Kendra said to the nurse.

"Ma'am, I'm sorry. Unless you're a relative, I cannot release any information," the nurse replied.

"I am a relative. That is my daughter's father," she said while sobbing.

"I'm sorry, ma'am, I suggest you ask the family that is waiting for an update," she said, looking over at me.

I was hoping that she has the sense enough to go sit

in the corner and not come this way with the bull, but who was I fooling? She was as dumb as a box of rocks.

"Budah, please tell me that Mari is okay," she said.

Before he could open his mouth, Robi was right there ready to go in. "Bitch, if you don't get your raggedy ass from around here trying to act all concerned about my son, I know something!" Robi shouted.

"I just came to check on my baby daddy," she replied.

While she and Robi continued to argue, Justice came from behind the locked emergency doors. She was a mess. There was blood everywhere, and she was sobbing uncontrollably.

"Justice, are you okay?" I asked.

"They wouldn't let me see him," she replied.

At this point, I had enough. We had been waiting for what seemed like hours to hear something from someone. Walking over to the nurse's station, I asked to speak with whoever was in charge. The nurse stared at me like I had two heads, and that was when I lost it.

"I need to speak with whoever is in charge! We have been waiting hours, and no one in the damn hospital has brought their ass out to speak with the family yet! Now, you have six minutes to get someone out in front of us, or I will go back there my damn self and find someone!" I shouted.

This bitch was so busy watching Kairo that she wasn't doing her job.

"Oh, and you can take your eyes off him because you damn sure don't want me to get mad. So I advise you to do your fucking job," I stated.

When I turned around, everyone was staring at me like I had three heads.

"What y'all staring at? Y'all know you wanted to do that so hush," I said to them.

The next thing I knew, there was a doctor calling for the family. As we gathered in the waiting room, Kairo asked if we could go somewhere private to speak with the doctor. Taking us into a private family area, the doctor started off with Kamari was alive.

"Mr. Richardson was shot three times—once in the shoulder and twice on his left side. I'm assuming he received those from shielding his girlfriend. The wounds to his side missed a lot of his vital organs, and we were able to remove the bullets with no issue. I would like to keep him here for a day or two, just to make sure there are no reactions to the meds and the stitches. I had him placed under an alias, as instructed by the detective on the case," he said.

"I appreciate everything you're doing for my brother. When can we see him?" Kairo asked.

"Give me a couple more minutes to get him moved into his room, and I'll have a nurse come and get you guys," he replied.

"Thank you again for everything," Robi said.

"You're welcome, ma'am," he replied and left out.

Once everyone cleared out of the room, leaving Kairo and myself still there, taking a seat next to him, I rubbed his shoulder while he sat with his head down looking at the floor.

"You okay, bae?" I asked.

"I can't lose my brother, bae. He is all that I have left that has the same blood running through our veins. Now that I know that he is okay, these niggas about to learn what real pain is," he stated.

"Okay... I'm not sure what that means, but please don't get hurt," I replied

"I'm not; they are. Over the next couple days, you are going to be exposed to a couple of things and a couple of people. I trust you, so that is the reason why you will be exposed to these things," he stated

"Okay," I replied. I was completely lost because it was like he was talking in codes to me or something.

"Detective McCray works for us," he said.

"Okay. I was wondering how he knew to move Mari and have him listed under another name," I responded.

"Asha, I have plans for the future, and come hell or high water, you will be in it. You are the only woman that I have truly let my guard down for. If this isn't the life for you, let me know now before you get in too deep, because there is no turning back after that," he said.

"Well, I have always loved a challenge," I said with a grin.

Walking out of the room, Kendra was still standing there looking mad as hell because no one would tell her anything about Mari.

"Kendra, go home, man. No one has time for your bullshit, and no one is gonna tell you anything," Kairo said.

I was tired of her shit, and I wasn't about to sit here and watch her keep fucking with everyone with her ugly ass. I calmly walked over to the nurse's station and spoke with the new nurse that was there and asked her to call security to have Kendra's ass removed. It took them all of five minutes to appear and walk out of the door, telling her that if she came back, she would be arrested.

"I like the way you move, Asha," Robi said, laughing.

"I'm sick of her ass," I replied.

As we all got onto the elevator to go see Mari, when we got to the floor, Justice took off running down the hall like a big ass kid and turned into where there was a man sitting in a chair outside of a room. By the time that we made it into the room, Justice and Miya were curled up in Mari's bed. It was the funniest thing ever. Here they both were in the bed like a bunch of crybabies.

"Get y'all asses out that damn bed. Got my baby all scrunched up," Robi said.

"They straight, Ro," Mari said.

"I'm not going to stay too long. I have to get back to the house to get Blessing," Robi said.

"Asha, can you go to the house and bring me some clothes to change into?" Justice asked.

"Yeah, I'll bring you some. Is there anything else y'all want?" I asked.

"Yeah, a nigga hungry," Mari said.

"I'll go by and get y'all some food. Text me what you want," Tez said.

"Aye, who's the chick?" Mari asked.

"Monica, is that you?" Justice yelled.

"Live and in the flesh, boo," Monica said.

"OMG, it has been too long. How you ended up here?" she asked.

"I was hanging out with Louise here, and you know trouble had to find us." She laughed.

I was watching Tez the whole time that Justice and Monica talked. He had his eyes fixated on her. I hoped he knew that dealing with her, I wouldn't hesitate to kick his and any bitch's ass.

"Well, let's head over to the house to get them something to change into so we can head to the house. My head is starting to hurt," I said.

Saying our goodbyes and telling Monica I would call her later, we headed to Mari's and Justice's places so we could get them some clothes. Mari's house was about ten minutes away from the hospital. When we pulled up, the doorman told Kairo that some guys had come looking for Mari a couple days ago and was asking what kind of car he drove. He told him that he didn't give them any information and was going to tell Mari but hadn't seen him since.

When we made it into the house, Kairo was mad all over again. Taking out his phone, he went to sending texts and calling people.

"McCray, I need you to pull the surveillance camera from Kamari's condo. The doorman just told me some niggas was asking about him outside his building," he said into the phone.

"Go ahead and get them some clothes so we can head back to the hospital," he said to me.

"Hell, I have to call them because I don't know where anything is," I said.

Taking my phone out my purse, I saw that Justice had texted me a list of stuff and where to find everything. Following the list, I grabbed a Gucci bag and put their stuff in it. I grabbed Justice's bookbag, and we were ready to leave.

Getting back into the car with Kairo, he still was mad. I wanted to say something to him, but I didn't want to bother him and his thoughts. Once we got back to the hospital, Kairo waited in the car while I ran up to drop their things off. Justice was still in the place that I left her, right beside Kamari, and they both were sleep.

Getting back into the car, we headed to the house. My body and head was hurting, so I leaned the seat back so that I could relax.

"Bae, we have to get your car," I said.

"Blaze went and picked it up for me," he replied.

I didn't realize I was sleeping until Kairo picked me up and carried up into the house and to our bedroom. When he put me down, I went immediately to the bathroom to turn on the Jacuzzi. The water felt so good on my sore body. Kairo returned with a bottle of water and three Aleve.

"I have to make me an appointment to take my hair out. I got blood and grass in it," I said.

"Call and make an appointment for tomorrow. I'll pay for it," he replied.

I'll text her when I get out," I replied.

I sat in the Jacuzzi for about thirty minutes before deciding to get out and cook something to eat. Throwing on some tights and a sports bra, I walked past the mirror when I noticed my bruised back. Turning around so that I could get a better view of my back, it was completely black and blue. Just the sight of my back made me want to jump in the car and go looking for Ameka and the chick, Mona, like I would in my younger days. Thank God for growth, but please don't let me see them, because I wouldn't be responsible for what happened.

Walking down the stairs, I went into the kitchen to find something to eat. I had a taste for some salmon, and I had just bought some fresh the other day. Taking out what I needed for dinner, I turned on Pandora and connected it to the speaker in the entertainment room. Kairo was sitting on the patio watching the dogs, smoking a cigar, and having a drink.

I was now in my cooking zone. I opened a bottle of wine and went to work. I had a recipe that I wanted to try out that would work great with the salmon and the asparagus that I was cooking.

"What the fuck is wrong with your back!" Kairo yelled, startling me out of my zone.

"What?" I asked.

"Tell me that those bitches didn't cause this?" He slammed his drink on the counter hard enough to break it.

When I turned to face him, he had this look of death on his face, and it scared the shit out of me. Taking his phone out of his back pocket , he started taking pictures of my back. He sent them to someone, and the next thing I knew, his phone was ringing.

"I want everyone that was there while this fight took place lined up in front of me in forty-eight hours! Don't make me get out in these fucking streets, because I'm killing everything moving!" he shouted.

I had never seen this side of him. There was anger, rage, and a bit of crazy in his eyes, and it had me scared shitless.

"What you are cooking in here, beautiful?" he asked.

Just like that, he had returned to the person that I had known all this time.

"Ummm, are you okay?" I asked, biting my lip.

"Yeah. Seeing those bruises did something to me. I didn't mean to scare you," he said, hugging me.

"So I'm cooking salmon with a brown-sugar glaze,

bacon-wrapped asparagus, and mashed red potatoes," I said, peeling the potatoes.

"Good, 'cause a nigga hungry as shit," he stated.

As he went to sit at the island in the kitchen, the doorbell rang. Getting up to answer the door, I heard loud ass Tez coming in talking shit.

"Damn! Asha got it smelling right in here," he said.

"Yeah, I need to send my wife over here for cooking lessons. That damn woman will burn a boiled egg if she could." Blaze laughed.

"You sure can send her over. I learned to cook from the best," I replied.

"Y'all bring y'all greedy asses on. Begging for food and shit," Kairo said.

"Asha, what's up with ya girl though?" Tez asked.

"Nope, not going to happen. You won't have my friend out here looking like a duck and whipping bitches' asses behind you," I replied.

"Damn, Ash. Don't do him like that," Kairo said.

"You be quiet. I didn't even do anything to ole psycho ass Ameka, and she runs behind me jumping me and shit," I said.

"Man, if I were you, I would try again at a later time," Blaze said, laughing.

When they went out on the patio, I went ahead and texted Monica just to see what she would say about Tez.

Me: Hey, girl!

Mo: Ash, how are you feeling?

Me: I've been better.

Mo: We can always go and find them bitches and beat their ass one by one. LOL!

Me: That doesn't sound half bad. So... Tez asked about you.

Mo: *You mean lil' sexy?*

Me: *Girl, you think he's cute?*

Mo: *Yes, he looks like he can do a couple things too LOL!*

Me: *OMG! Here I am telling him he isn't your type, and your ass all in!*

Mo: *Yep, hand him my number.*

I had to shake my head at Monica. She was still the same ole crazy person that I had known in school. I was glad that we had run into each other at the school.

Going back to what I was doing, I noticed that Kairo was now standing up and looking at something on his laptop. The next thing I knew, he was raising his voice to Blaze and Tez. I wasn't sure what it was, but the look on his face told me that he wasn't happy. I was somewhat scared to stick my head out the door to tell them to come make their plates because I didn't want to interrupt what they were doing. I had everything set out, so the only thing they had to do was fix their plate while I had Kairo's waiting for him on the counter. My body was starting to hurt again, so I headed upstairs with my plate to take something and lie down.

BUDAH

Of all the shit that I'd been through, I never thought I'd ever have to worry about someone coming for my family. Saying that I was pissed was an understatement. I was seeing red from the moment shit went down with Asha and then Mari and Justice. I could tell that Asha was walking on eggshells around me, but I really wasn't pissed off at her. Ameka, on the other hand, was going to feel everything that I was going through when they finally caught up to her ass. I couldn't blame Asha for fighting this time. As much as I didn't want her to, she had no choice but to defend herself.

I didn't even realize she was a beast with her hands and was holding her own until her sorry excuse of a mother hit her in the back of her head and knocked her out. Her homegirl Monica was a beast too. I could tell that the two of them raised a lot of hell when they were growing up.

It was so much going on in my head that it was starting to hurt. Asha's mother was going to die for the simple fact that she wasn't loyal. With a mother like that, who needs enemies, and for that, her and Ameka's lives were coming to an end soon. She didn't deserve to have the love of Justice and Asha. They were better off without her anyway. As I sat on the patio watching the dogs relieve themselves, I just shook my head at everything that had unfolded with her. What type of mother would side with a stranger and then cause harm that could've killed her own child? That gave a new meaning of "I brought you here, and I will take you out," as mothers say.

Tez and Blaze came over to show me the video that was floating around the neighborhood. I was pissed the fuck off as I watched the way her mother came from behind and hit her and took off running the other way. They also told me that Mari's shooting was retaliation from the other night when they ended up shooting some nigga.

I guess their boss didn't like the fact one of his soldiers didn't return home. What did he expect though? You're coming for niggas that have had these streets on lock for the last ten plus years and think that we are just going to hand it over to you because you think that you are applying pressure? Nah. We are built Ford tough, and we learned from the best, so I hope they were ready for this war they just started.

Blaze and Tez had left about thirty minutes ago, and I was now in the kitchen cleaning up. I didn't mind. Hell, I was surprised that Asha got up and cooked dinner. I knew she was hurting because she was moving around slowly, so once she made my plate and went upstairs, I knew it was a wrap for her.

I locked the house, set the alarm, and went upstairs to find Asha sleeping with her clothes still on. Taking off her tights, I slipped her under the covers and sat in a chair by the balcony doors and watched her sleep. She didn't know it, but I had pictures of her sleeping in my phones. She was so beautiful and peaceful. After watching for about ten minutes, I went and took me a shower and curled up under her and fell asleep.

When I woke up the following morning, Asha wasn't in the bed. Getting up to relieve myself, she was sitting in the Jacuzzi with her headphones in. She didn't even hear me come into the bathroom because they were so loud. When I finished, I stepped out of my boxers and joined her in the warm, bubbly water. She had bubbles everywhere.

"Shit, you scared me," Asha said.

Moving her closer so that I could place her on my lap, she took out her earbuds.

"Are you mad at me?" she asked.

"Nah, I'm not mad at you. You had to do what you had to do to defend yourself. I can't be mad at you for that. You a beast with them hands though," I said jokingly.

Kissing her softly while I lifted her onto my already erect wood, she let out a soft moan as she eased herself down onto me. She began to wind her hips into a circulation motion. Taking her breasts into my mouth, I sucked on each of them, paying special attention to the nipple. I was trying my best to be easy with her because I knew that she was sore, but she was bucking so hard. I had to get control of her. Lifting her up and stepping out of the shower, I sat her on the countertop and went as deep as I could inside of her. I could tell that she was about to cum because her moans became louder.

As she was getting close to her peak, she began to dig her nails into my shoulder. Taking her again, I moved over to the bench that I had sitting in the corner. Putting her down so that I could bend her over the end of the bench, I began to murder her beautiful, pink pussy. If I was one of those niggas that believed in recording having sex, I would damn sure record her. Her ass was nice and round. She had the perfect arch, not that lazy shit them chicks be doing. She stood on her tippy-toes so that she could meet each and every one of my thrusts.

Now taking her to the bed, I laid her on her back and proceeded to go as deep as I could. I wanted her to feel all eleven inches that I was giving her.

"Ah, shit," she moaned.

"What, bae?" I asked.

"Shit, you better not," she said as her eyes rolled in the back of her head.

Flipping her again, onto her stomach, I went in deep from the back. I knew she was probably hurting right now, but I wanted all of her.

"Oh, shit... I'm about to cum," she said.

Inserting my thumb into her ass, she squirted all over the covers. While she was finished, I wasn't quite done with her yet. I was hungry, and she was the only one that would feed me what I needed. Picking her up bridal style, I took her out on the patio and laid her on the chaise lounge. After giving her world-shattering orgasms and making her cum three times more, I was finally satisfied and released inside of her as she was riding me.

All the years of me fucking bitches, I never released

inside of them. It was either in their mouth or on them, but never inside of them. Lying next to each other naked in our sexual glow trying to catch our breaths, our moment was interrupted by my brother, Mari, calling.

"Nigga, what's up?" I asked.

"Nigga, why the fuck you outta breath? Never mind, man," Mari said.

"What's up?" I asked again.

"What time y'all coming up here? A nigga ready to go home," he stated.

I could hear Justice in the background talking shit about something.

"We will be up there in about forty-five minutes," I responded.

"Bring the baby, bro," he said and hung up.

Hanging up with him, Asha walked out of the bathroom looking sexy as shit.

"So you ready to carry my seeds?" I asked.

"Boy, stop playing," she replied.

"I'm not playing with you. I want you to be the mother of my children," I stated.

"And I want to be someone's wife, not a baby momma," she replied.

"Say less," I replied, walking into the bathroom to shower.

She didn't know that sliding a ring on her finger was in the plans. I just had to make sure that she wouldn't cave under pressure.

I wanted to be lazy today and just lounge around the house, but I knew I had shit to do, and that included getting to the bottom of who was responsible for trying to take out my family.

Taj, Kiah, and Night arrived last night, so I knew it was a matter of time before they showed their faces and got shit cracking.

"You call about your hair?" I asked.

"Yeah. Kia from Sheer Essence is coming to take this hair out tomorrow," she said.

"Ight," I replied.

After we finished getting dressed, we headed to Mari's house to get them some clothes. It took us about ten minutes to grab their stuff and be out the door. No sooner than we got back into the car, Robi texted me that she and Blessing were on their way to the hospital.

"Has Robi said anything about my father's people?" she asked.

"Nah. I'll ask her about it though," I replied.

We pulled up to the hospital and went up to Mari's room. As we were heading down the hall, all of a sudden, we heard yelling. Asha took off running, and I followed behind her.

"Bitch, I will break your fucking neck in this bitch!" Mari yelled.

"Fuck you! I come down here to check on your ass, and you got this rat-face bitch in here!" She hissed.

"Call me another bitch, and I will wipe the floor with your thot-bucket ass!" Justice shouted.

"Where the fuck is the guard?" Asha asked.

"I'm sorry, y'all. I stepped away to use the restroom," the guard said, returning to the scene of the commotion.

"Get her the fuck outta here before she ends up in here herself," I stated.

Just as she was being walked down the hall, Robi,

Miya, and Blessing stepped out of the elevator, giving her another reason to show her ass about something.

"I can't believe y'all took my baby from me and won't let me see her!" she shouted.

"If you don't get your poor-looking ass from up here acting a damn fool, I know something," Robi said.

"This isn't the last that y'all heard of me," she said, getting on the elevator.

I hoped she didn't think that was a threat. I had a list of people whose lives would be ending soon, and I didn't mind adding her ass also.

I was about to call McCray about the guard, but he was already heading down the hallway toward me.

"I need to speak with you ASAP," he said.

"Bet. Meet me in the garage in twenty minutes," I replied.

"I want out of this motherfucker now!" Mari yelled.

"Man, calm down before you bust your stitches," I said.

"Man, I'm not with this shit. Kendra dumb ass comes up here with the bullshit, trying to flex and shit. Nah, I'm out this bitch," he said.

"If you don't calm all that rah-rah shit down, I'm going to bust a stitch my damn self," the voice behind us said.

Turning around, it was Kiah standing at the door.

"I'm trying to tell this nigga. What's up, bro?" I said.

"Ain't shit. I hope these lil' niggas ready," he replied.

"Come on, y'all. Let them talk," Robi said.

"Leave my niece here, Auntie," Kiah said.

"Taj and Night will get up with you later. You know

them niggas stay in business mode, so what's the scoop on these niggas?" Kiah asked.

"I got a feeling it's that nigga Boola or whatever his name is. Mari and Tez knocked off one of his soldiers the other day," I said.

"So you got some intel on this nigga or what?" Kiah asked.

"Yeah. I'm about to go meet with my dude now to see what he got for me," I responded.

"Well, nigga, let's go see what he has to say. Mari, we'll be back," Kiah said, setting Blessing down on the bed.

Taking the elevator to the parking garage, we met up with McCray. He had been working for me since he was a rookie on the force.

"Aye, what's good?" I asked.

"So dude you are looking for goes by the name of Nasir Robinson. He is small time but has been making a name for himself lately," McCray said.

"You think this nigga had something to do with the raids and the hit?" I asked.

"The raids? Nah, that's not him. I got a lil' honey working on that. The hit was definitely him though."

"Anything else? I asked.

"Yeah. He used to mess with ya girl back in the day," he said.

"Who?"

"Asha. She's clean though. They been stopped fucking around for some years. Couldn't keep his dick in his pants or his hands to himself," he stated.

"Ight. Let me know if you get more info."

McCray walked off and hopped into his car and pulled off.

"Yo, can you trust ya girl, man?" Kiah asked.

"Hell yeah, I can trust her. She hasn't asked for shit since I've been fucking with her," I stated.

"I'm just trying to make sure, man. Don't wanna catch you slipping about some pussy, ya feel me?" Kiah said.

We made our way back to Kamari's room where Blessing was now lying back on the bed doing her favorite thing. blowing bubbles.

"So what he had to say?" Mari asked.

"The dude supposed to be some over on the eastside cat that Asha used to mess with," I said.

"Oh, word? So she set me up?" he asked.

"Nigga, why the fuck would she set you up? The fuck Asha going to set you up and damn near get her sister killed in the process? You sound dumb as hell," I stated.

"I'm just saying, nigga. Don't beat me up," Mari said with a laugh.

"Nigga, fuck you." I had to laugh myself.

"Boy, that nigga feeling her bad, ready to bust you in your shit and all," Kiah said.

When the ladies returned, we stayed for about twenty more minutes before Asha and I left. The doctor had finally given in to Mari's demand of being let go with the instruction of not to get worked up. When Asha and I were driving home, I couldn't help but ask Asha about the nigga Nasir.

"Bae, you know some nigga named Nasir?" I asked.

"Ugh, I can't stand that hoe ass nigga. What about him?" she asked, seemingly shocked that I would bring him up.

"What happened between y'all two?" I asked.

"He couldn't keep his dick in his pants, and I was just

tired of the drama and the fighting with the random bitches," she stated.

"His name keeps coming up in a couple things that's going on. They think he might have something to do with the raid and the shooting," I stated.

"The raid I could see, because he does run his mouth a lot, but the shooting? He's too scary for that," she replied.

"If he had anything to do with anything, I promise his days are numbered," I said.

"Oh, well. That's his ass. Doesn't make a difference to me either way," she replied.

On the way back to the house, Robi called. Putting her on the speakerphone, I answered. "What's up, Ro?"

"Where's Asha?" she asked.

"I'm right here, Ro," she said.

"Hey, baby. I'm on my way to talk to your people tonight. I'll text you tonight when I get home," she said.

"Okay. I'll talk to you later," she replied.

"Are you nervous about what they will say?" I asked.

"Of course I am. What if they don't want to meet me because of my so-called mother?" she stated.

"Ash, you will be fine. If they don't want to be in your life, then fuck them," I said.

JUSTICE

I couldn't believe that this broad had the nerve to come back up here after she showed her ass yesterday trying to act concerned and shit. When she came in the hospital room, she didn't know that I was there. I had just got out of the shower and heard everything that she was saying. She was begging Mari to take her back so that they could be a family. She promised to take care of Blessing the correct way. Her whole tune changed when I walked out of the bathroom door.

"I can't believe you have me in here acting like you want your family back, all the while you have this bitch here too!" she yelled.

I couldn't do anything but laugh because the expression on her face was priceless. It wasn't until Mari asked her to leave that she really started showing her ass throwing shit. The icing on the cake was when she yelled that she was going back to court to get custody of Blessing. Even with Mari having stitches, he got out of the bed and pinned her against the wall.

"I'll fucking kill you before Blessing ever steps foot back into the house with you and your mom," he whispered so only the three of us could hear.

I was able to get him off her and get him seated back on the bed. As I was doing that, the bitch had the nerve to swing on me from behind. Here I was trying to save her dumb ass, and she swings on me.

"Have you lost your fucking mind?" I asked.

"You think that you're going to take my man, my child, and have the life I'm supposed to be living and think I'm cool with it!" she yelled.

"I'm trying to be cool, but keep playing with me, and I will mop the fucking floor with you in this room!" I yelled.

Before I knew it, Budah and Asha were coming through the door on one hundred.

"Bitch, didn't I tell your silly ass to stay the fuck away from my brother and don't come back up here? Now I have been wanting to murk your ass, and the only thing that has been saving your ass was Blessing, but since you don't have her, there really isn't anything stopping me is there," Budah calmly said.

"Hello? Justice?" Mari said.

"Yes. Sorry, bae," I said.

"Where were you?" he asked.

"I was just thinking about earlier and your crazy ass baby momma," I replied.

"Yeah, that shit was wild."

We had been home for about two hours now. Mari had raised enough hell about him wanting to go home that the doctor discharged him, against his better judgment. He did give Mari a prescription and orders not to move too fast to try to pick up anything. I was about to go to the store because there wasn't anything in the house, especially if Mari was going to be home.

"I'm about to head to the store. Do you want anything?" I asked.

"Nah. Look in the top dresser drawer. There is money and car keys up there," he replied.

I finished taking inventory of what we needed, making a list on my phone. In no time, I was out the door heading to the store. As I was walking down the aisle of the store, Drea called me.

"What's up, chick?" I asked.

"Don't 'what's up, chick' me! Why I have to hear in the street that Kamari car was shot up and that you and him were in the car?" she yelled, being dramatic and crying.

"OMG! If you don't stop that damn crying." I laughed.

"I don't find this funny, friend. I was worried as shit about you," she replied.

"Girl, stop. I'm fine. Kamari is home recovering," I stated.

"Where are you now?" she asked.

"I'm at the store getting groceries for the house. Mari's house doesn't have anything in it."

"So when can I come to see you to judge if you're okay?" she asked.

"I'll plan something soon. Maybe we will do lunch or something."

"Alright. Well, let me get back to work. Lunch break is just about over," she said.

We said our goodbyes, and I finished getting the final

items that I needed before heading to checkout. I did feel bad though. Since I had been dealing with Kamari, I hadn't spent any time with Drea, just random texts every so often. Checking all the items that I had bought and put into the trunk of the car, I headed back to the house. As I was pulling the car into the garage, I saw Tez getting out of his truck.

"Shit. I thought you were Mari driving. I was about to curse your ass out," he said.

"Nope, it's just me," I said as opened the truck door.

"My bad. Let me get the bags from you," he said, grabbing the bags.

We walked into the building. When we made it to the door, I heard a voice from the other side. Opening the door, it was Blessing, Miya, and Robi in the house. Robi was in the kitchen cooking something that smelled wonderful.

"Robi, I didn't know that you guys were coming over," I said.

"I figured I would come over and cook you guys a meal. I know that you have final exams coming up, and you need to study," she stated.

Miya took the bags that Tez had in his hands and unpacked them and put the stuff up. I sat at the counter while I watched Robi cook on the other side. I was tired as hell from not sleeping in the hospital. They had one of those pullout beds, but they were just as uncomfortable as the chairs that they had.

"Justice, you look tired. Why don't you go and lay down until the food is done?" she said.

Taking her suggestion, I went into the bedroom with

a book that I needed to finish for an exam that I was having next week. I took me a nice, hot shower to relax before I started reading. I don't think I made it to the third page before I was knocked out. I was sleeping good as hell until I felt little hands on my face and slob. Opening my eyes, it was Blessing on top of me, trying to wake me up. Mari was lying on the bed watching SportsCenter.

"Hey, beautiful," he said.

"Hey. How long have I been asleep?" I asked.

"Couple hours," he replied.

"OMG! Why did you let me sleep that long?" I asked.

"Robi told me not to wake you, that you needed your rest," he replied.

"Is everyone gone?" I asked.

"Yeah, been gone for a while. Robi said that she left your plate in the microwave."

Getting up off the bed, I walked into the kitchen and retrieved the plate that Robi had left in the kitchen. She made fried pork chops, mac and cheese, and corn. I couldn't walk up the stairs because I was trying to eat. Coming back into the room, I sat on the side of the bed where Blessing crawled to me. Blowing the mac and cheese so that I could give her some, Mari tried to grab her.

"Blessing, no."

"Leave her alone. She is fine," I said.

"She already ate, Just. She's not hungry, just greedy."

"That's fine too. Let the baby eat," I replied.

I finished my food and went to take the plate to the kitchen. When I returned, Mari had put Blessing in her crib and turned on the monitor so we could hear her. She was in the room making sounds and talking in her language. He was leaned against the headboard looking like a whole meal, and I just ate.

"Stop looking at me like that. We already had this conversation, and you ain't ready," he said.

"How am I looking?" I questioned.

"Like you want a sample of this dick. I promise you, this dick will fuck up your world," he stated.

Going into the bathroom to wash my face and hands, my mind wondered what it would feel like to have him inside of me. Drying my face and hands, I walked back into the room and lay back on my side of the bed to watch what he was looking at. Mari stood up and went to the foot of the bed, where he grabbed the one foot that I had where he was now standing. Still lying down, he hovered over me while kissing me softly. Moving from my lips, he went to my collar bone, and then my ear, setting my whole body on fire.

Sitting me up, he gently removed my sports bra over my head, exposing my pierced 36D breasts. He continued to kiss on my collarbone while traveling down to my breasts, taking his time on each one of them. He planted soft kisses, traveling down my stomach to my hips. Lifting so that he would be able to remove the tights that I was wearing, he looked up to me for approval before he removed them. Nodding my head, he went ahead and removed the tights, revealing my now-wet pussy.

Kneeling so that he was eye to eye with my pussy while getting as close as he could, he inhaled my scent. Taking my pussy lips, he spread them and gently blew on my pearl. Letting out a light moan, I began to squirm. He slid one of his fingers inside of me while he sucked on my clit. He stayed there for a while, telling me that he wasn't going to stop until I came on his face. I tried to buck and scoot away from him. That only had him intensify the pressure that he was putting on my clit. He stood to his feet and pulled me up to switch positions, telling me to sit on his face. I was scared and unsure because I didn't want to suffocate him.

"Come on, Justice. I will be fine," he assured me.

He bunched all of the pillows, so he was comfortable, and lay back on the bed, climbing on top of him until I was standing on top of him. Guiding me down so I was centered with his face, I began to ease myself down. Once I was in a position where he was comfortable, he locked down on my hips so that I couldn't go anywhere. His mouth felt so good that I found myself grabbing my own titties, which I found out turned me on even more.

Before I knew it, the floodgates were opened, and I was riding his face like a horse.

"Yeah, Justice... let that shit go just like that," he said as I continued.

Climaxing on top of him, my whole body jerked in ecstasy. Rolling over so I was now lying on my back, I noticed his erect dick. Although I was a virgin, I had been told by the few people I had done it to that I had a lethal ass head game. Mari was now scrolling through his phone. This could go two ways. He would either lie back and let me do what I do, or he would think that I was lying about being a virgin and curse my ass out.

Making my way down to his dick, I unleashed this beautiful beast out of his boxers

"Justice, come on. You have no idea what to do with that. Don't play games with me," he said.

Not saying a word to him, I proceeded to deep throat his entire dick. Coming back up, I eyed him as he watched me. Spitting on the top of his wood, I went to work with my mouth and hands.

"Shit, what the fuck, Justice?" he moaned.

When he said that, I knew I had him right where I wanted him—time to put on a show. I let out light moans as I made hand movements like a pepper grinder.

"Fuck, Justice," he moaned again.

I figured if I wasn't going to give him any pussy yet, the least I could do was fuck his head up with this fire ass head of mine. After about eight minutes, he started to push me away. I knew what that meant; he was about to cum. Just as I was moving away, he released loads of cum down his hand.

Getting out of the bed, he walked to the bathroom to wash his hands. Coming out of the bathroom, he had this crazy ass look on his face, and I knew what the next question would be.

"Justice, where in the fuck did you learn to suck dick like that?" he asked.

Oh, shit! He is pissed! I said to myself.

"I did have a boyfriend before you. Although weren't fucking, he did show me what he liked," I replied.

"Nah, b. You don't get that good just off one nigga. Tell the truth. You been lying to me about being a virgin?" he asked.

"Mari, as bad as I wanted to have you inside of me, the answer is no. No one has ever been inside of me," I replied.

"My bad, Just. I can't imagine a nigga getting head like this on a regular and not want to slide inside of you," he said.

"Hence, the reason we broke up," I stated.

Cuddling up to him, I drifted off to la-la land in his arms.

MARI

Justice had me all fucked up with that little show she just put on. Who the fuck had been receiving this fiyah ass head and didn't appreciate it? Just thinking about that shit made me want to find the nigga and murk his ass for trying my baby like that. As bad as I wanted to dig into her guts after that, I knew that I had to take my time and be patient with her.

As I laid there watching SportsCenter, I thanked God for allowing me to pull through the shooting. I wanted to be there for Blessing, and come hell or high water, I was going to do that. I had been thinking about my next move. Kairo and I didn't have a chance to take while I was in the hospital. I'd see him later. Especially with Kiah being here, I knew it would be a matter of time before the others made it here. I hoped they know what type of problems were ahead of them.

Looking over at Justice, her ass was going to school in the morning. She had been out for a couple days, but it's back to school she goes. No one was going to say once she started fucking with me, she stopped going to school. She has two months left in school, and she was going to finish out strong and walk across the stage to get her diploma. I wanted to take her on a trip once she did that, maybe to the Bahamas or something. Setting my alarm so that it would wake us up for school, I went to check on Blessing, and she knocked out cold I still can't believe that Kendra dumb ass hadn't been taking care of my baby they way that she should have. All she had to do was keep her straight and she was set, but no she was so worried about being with me she harmed my child like that was going to make us get back together. If anything it was going to get her ass killed fucking with my baby.

The alarm went off at six a.m., and I leaned over to wake up Justice.

"Justice, get up, bae."

"Where am I going, Kamari?" she asked.

"You got school. Get up."

"I'm not going," she replied.

"Justice, get your ass up. You have two months left. Now is not the time to fuck it up. You can go on your own, or I can help you, but you're going," I said, turning on the lights.

"I want to stay with you," she whined.

"I'll be here. I'm not going anywhere. Now go ahead and get dressed."

Snatching the covers off her, she stomped into the bathroom pouting. I didn't care, as long as she carried her ass to school. Getting out of the bed, I went to check on Blessing. She was in the crib playing with her feet, looking at the toy hanging above her. Picking her up, I grabbed her diapers and wipes. By the time I made it out the living room, Justice was just turning on the shower, and I heard Pandora playing.

Changing Blessing, I turned on cartoons while I went into the kitchen to fix her a bottle and me a cup of coffee. By the time that I was finished, Justice came from out of the room, still pouting about having to go to school.

"It's some money on the counter by your purse. Have a good day," I said, kissing her lips.

She walked over to Blessing and kissed her and left out of the house. It was still early, so I would wait to call Kairo because he would curse my ass out. That nigga hates being woken up for anything but would wake a nigga out their sleep for dumb shit. Just as I was about to doze off, birdbrain called me.

"What, man?" I asked.

"So you really aren't going to let me see my baby?" she asked.

"Hell nah, you aren't going to see her. Fuck I look like? Your ass couldn't take care of her when you had her. Now, all of a sudden, you so worried about her," I said.

"Please! We can meet at a park. Just a couple minutes," she begged.

"I'll think about it and hit you back," I responded, hanging up.

I sent Justice a text asking her what she thought about it. She said that the goal was to never keep Blessing from her but to get her in a better environment. She also told me that if decided, take Asha just in case she wanted to buck. Asha wouldn't hesitate to pop her ass. Taking heed to what she said, I texted Asha to see if she was up.

Me: Asha, you up?
Sis: Yeah, what's up?

Me: I need a favor. Can you come scoop me?"
Sis: Give me about thirty minutes.
Me: Ight.

Texting Kendra what park to be at in forty-five minutes, I started to get Blessing and myself dressed. By the time that Asha was ringing the doorbell, I had just finished getting dressed and just needed to put on my shoes.

"What's up, bro?" she said, picking up Blessing

"I need you to run to the park so Kendra can see Blessing," I said.

"Ummm, why would I do that?" she asked.

"Because Justice told me to take you instead of going by myself."

"Look, I'll take y'all, but the moment she starts popping big shit, I'm going to pop her right in her shit," she replied.

"Well, we are going to hope she doesn't, Laila Ali," I said, laughing.

The park was about ten minutes from the house, so when we pulled up, Kendra and her mom were waiting on the bench. Getting out, Asha pulled out her stroller as Monica pulled up.

"Damn, Ash, you brought backup?" I laughed.

"You think this shit funny. I play no games with these hoes," she said, putting Blessing in the stroller.

"We gonna stay back here, but the first loud voice, it's a wrap," Monica said.

Walking over to where Kendra and Kitty were, they immediately started talking shit about what Blessing had on.

"Why you got my baby dressed like a boy?" she said with an attitude.

Not paying her any mind, I stood in front of them as they played with Blessing.

"What kind of man are you to take a child from their mother?" Kitty asked.

"I'm a man that will not allow anyone to treat my child any kind of way, the fuck you thought?" I responded.

"You didn't even want her to begin with!" Kendra yelled, crying.

"We have a problem here?" Asha said out of nowhere.

"What the fuck you come over here like you going to do something!" Kitty shouted.

"I'm here to make sure my brother is straight, that's it. I would hate his good act to have a different outcome," Asha said.

I watched as Asha handled Kitty and Kendra in a way that would make my brother proud. She was cool, calm, and collected, not raising her voice one to get her point across.

"That's enough time for us to go," I said.

I took Blessing out of Kendra's hands before this shit went left and Kairo blame me for Asha out here in the park fighting. As we got back into the truck, we headed toward Kairo's house. When we made it to Kairo's house, there were cars in the driveway that were familiar, which meant Kiah and the crew had touched down. I grabbed Blessing and Asha got her bag, and we walked into the house to be met by Kairo, Kiah, Taj, Tez, and Midnight.

"What's up, lil' nigga?" Taj said.

"Man, fuck all that. Give me my niece," Midnight said.

"Hey, gangsta," Kairo said to Asha.

"Oh, this the fighter, huh?" Midnight asked.

"Yeah, this her," Kairo said, giving Asha a look.

"Oh, she will fit in with the other ladies just fine then," Midnight said.

"Man, listen, Keta is the ass kicker of the bunch, but these two lit some shit up too," he said, pointing at Asha and Monica.

"Ash, can you watch Blessing while I go talk to the fellas?" I asked.

"Of course I will," she said.

As soon as we closed the door to the office, Midnight wanted details on everything.

"So what's the deal on this nigga?" Midnight asked.

"So we found out who is responsible for the hit the other day on Mari. Some no-name nigga named Nasir, I have to find out his last name," Tez said.

"Hold on, let me ask Asha," Kairo said.

Leaving out of the office, everyone looked crazy when Kairo said he was going to ask Asha. When he returned, Taj and Midnight looked at her for an answer.

"His last name is Robinson. He used to fuck with Asha some years ago," he said.

"So let me ask you something," Midnight said.

"No, she doesn't have anything to do with the hit or the raid on my house. In fact, she can't stand the nigga's guts," he said.

"You sure she can be trusted?" Taj asked.

"Yeah, I'm sure," he said.

"So who this nigga working for then?" Midnight asked.

"That, I can't find out. Nobody knows that," Tez said.

Without saying anything else, he took out his phone and dialed a number.

"Mills, I need everything that you have on a Nasir Robinson. I want everything: mom's name, dad's name—hell, I want to know what the nigga had from lunch yesterday," he said, hanging up.

We sat around in the office and talked shit to one another while we waited to see if any information would come in from Mills. While we were waiting, Blaze came in with some information also.

"What is it, Blaze?" I asked.

"Can't call it. If you guys here, then I know some shit about to pop off," she said.

"Not yet. Just making sure everyone straight," Midnight said.

"So the word going around is that someone in the crew has been talking with the state," she said.

"So who are they saying is talking with them?" Kairo asked.

"They are saying that Tyshawn is the one talking," Blaze stated.

"Tez, did you ever hear anything from-ole girl at the DA's office?" I asked.

"Nah, let me hit her up right now," he replied.

"Yo, I know this nigga didn't set us up like that. Please tell me that this nigga didn't go against the grain over some bullshit charges," Kairo said.

"I don't know, bro, but we definitely will find out," Blaze said**Budah**

"I know this nigga didn't eat off my family for years, only to turn his back on us when shit got shaky. I paid this nigga's mom's house off because I love her to death, and she was struggling to stay afloat. Gave this nigga money for child support, X-mas gifts, baby showers, and DNA tests, and this is what this soft cake ass nigga do?" I was fuming.

"Man, this nigga got to get dealt with ASAP," Mari said.

I know he felt bad also because he went hard for him when he first started out. He was right too. He was solid and a true shoulder, so I wondered what made him turn against us.

Walking out of the room, I sent a text to McCray that I needed to meet him at Broadway in twenty. Broadway was a spot under the bridge that he and I knew about. The spot was off in the cut. No one could see the cars enter or exit the location. Letting everyone know that I would be back in a minute, I headed to the location to meet McCray.

As I was leaving out, Kia was getting out of the car with her supplies to do Asha's hair. Waiting for her, I showed her to the basement where Asha and Monica were, and then I headed out to meet with McCray. When I arrived, McCray was already there, sitting in his car eating.

"What's up?" he said.

"So the word on the streets is that Tyshawn is working for the state," I said.

"Tyshawn? Say word. That nigga know better. I haven't heard anything, but I damn sure will go hit up my friend in the DA's office and see what I can find out," he replied.

"You do that, and let me know what you come up with. If there is anyone else's name you see I need to know about, let me know too so they all can be dealt with at once," I stated.

We parted ways, and I headed back to the house. Before I got out of the car, I called McCray to see if he could find out any information on Kandi and Ameka also. Going back into the house, everyone was now on the porch smoking cigars and having a couple drinks. I ran downstairs to see if Asha would go ahead and order some food for us. She was just finishing up with her hair. It was long, as usual, and beautiful curls all over.

"Bae, will you order some food?" I asked.

"Yeah, what do you have a taste for?" she asked.

Licking my lips, I had a taste for something, and only she would be able to satisfy. I told her to come upstairs real quick. I wanted to talk to her about something. Following me up the stairs, we went into my office, where I cleared the top of my desk and laid her on it. Pulling her tights down enough for me to reach my prize, her bare pussy was showing, causing my manhood to stand at attention. Her moistness was visible on her lips. Licking her lips, it tasted sweet. Feasting on her, she squirmed on the desk, and I devoured her. Once she climaxed on the desk, I stood her up and sat on the couch against the wall. As she took her tights off, she straddled me and began to slowly ride me. It was like we were in our own world, and no one else existed. Even with everyone in the house, it was like they weren't.

As I was coming close to releasing, Asha was also getting close.

"Shit, I'm about to cum," she said.

"Let it go, baby. I'm about to bust," I said.

No sooner than I said that, Asha squirted all over me, the furniture, and floor.

"Oh, shit, bae. I made a mess," she said.

"Hell yeah, you did," I said.

"Stay right there. I'll go get you some clean clothes," she said.

Walking into my bathroom in the office, I turned the shower on while Asha returned with a change of clothes and cleaning supplies. When she was finished, I heard her and Monica talking shit to each other. Monica was calling her a hot ass while Asha was telling her she had to get it whenever. I walked out of the office, and Monica gave me the side-eye as I kissed Asha. Yeah, I didn't have a problem showing my affection for Asha because it was returned. She didn't care about the money, cars, or the name. She clearly showed me that she was about to make her own, so she wasn't impressed, or so she put on.

Justice was walking through the door as I was heading to the patio with the fellas.

"What's up, Justice? How was school?" I asked.

"It was straight," she replied.

Walking onto the patio, the fellas was listening to Taj tell one of his crazy ass stories with Keta. She was giving his ass a run for his money. I told him it was payback from all the females he had put through it. On top of that, he had a little girl that he had wrapped around his finger.

"I remember Yah and I used to steal time away from the group to have sex," Midnight said.

"It's just something about her. I just had to have her right there at that moment," I replied.

"Yeah, I know the feeling, my guy. That is how we

ended up with the three that I have now," he said, laughing.

I couldn't wait until Asha had my children. Although she didn't believe me, she was going to be my wife once this was all over. I wanted to be the first person she saw in the morning and the last person before she went to sleep. I wanted to be that extra father with my children at all the football games, fussing at the coaches.

"Aye, my nigga, you going to feed us or nah? I'm hungry as shit," Taj said.

No sooner than I said that, Asha and Monica came from out of the kitchen. She had whipped up something really quick until the food arrived. Kissing me on the cheek, she went back into the house with Monica and Justice. Pouring myself a drink, I got a text from McCray.

MC: No location on Kandi, but Ameka has been at her sister's house.

Me: Text me the address of the sister.

MC: Coming your way now.

When I received the address, I forwarded it over to Tez so that he could get a couple guys to watch the house. I was now trying to find out where Kandi's cokehead ass was at. She didn't have too many places that she could go. I had people sitting on her house, and she hadn't been seen coming or going out of there. It was so bad that Joe was also looking for her. He had gotten word of what she had done to Asha and was pissed as shit.

"So I want to try and have a sit-down with this nigga and see if we could be civilized about this before we start an all-out war, which I don't give a fuck about," Midnight said.

"Who finna talk to that nigga? The only thing I want

to hear is 'please don't kill me' before I let the gun ring out," I said.

"Give me the word, and we can get this shit started tonight," Kiah said.

"Tez, you know the blocks, right?" I asked.

"Each and every one of them," he said.

We had about a hundred-plus soldiers, so going to war could be easy because we could overpower them.

"The food is here," Monica said from the sliding door.

I could see the way that Monica was looking at Tez, and I knew she was feeling him just as much as he was feeling her. We all walked into the house. Justice was feeding Blessing and doing her homework. I was glad that she went back to school. She didn't need to stay and take care of Mari. He was a grown ass man.

"Just, you heard anything back from any of those schools you applied to?" Asha asked.

"Nah, my counselor said I should be hearing something from them in the next week or so. I have to call Miya and see if she has," she replied.

While everyone was eating, I received a text from McCray that Tyshawn was the leak and was cooperating with the state because he got caught with a minor a couple months ago. There really wasn't any information or any evidence other than the weed that they found in the house, and the junkies said it was theirs. He also said that he had a memo out looking for Kandi since none of his contacts hadn't seen her.

I think that I was more so hurt than pissed because I had invested so much into him, only to be slapped in the face. I was so angry that I punched the nearest wall, causing everyone to stop eating and look at me.

"Bro, you straight?" Mari asked.

"Yeah, I'm cool," I replied.

As everyone went back to eating, Robi called. I took her call outside on the patio.

"You home?" she asked.

"Yeah, I'm home with everyone," I replied.

"Who is everyone?" she asked.

"Mari, Justice, Blessing, Monica, Taj, Kiah, Tez, Blaze, and Midnight," I said.

"Well, I will call Asha a little while later when things settle down. I'm going to send Miya to get Blessing in a little," she said.

"Ight," I replied.

After everyone was finished eating, we sat around and came up with a strategy of how we wanted to handle these niggas. It had been a good five or six days since the incident with Justice and Mari. I knew their ass would be caught off guard when we hit them. I had Tez assemble a team and had them meet me that the warehouse tomorrow morning. Once we agreed on that, everyone said goodnight and went our separate ways.

ASHA

As I was cleaning the house after everyone left, I noticed that Monica and Tez were still out on the patio. Giving them time to talk while I finished inside the house, Kairo came over to get all the trash together so that he could empty it.

"What about taking a trip once everything settles down?" he asked.

"A trip sounds good right about now. There has been so much shit going on. I just need a getaway to relax," I said.

"Did Robi call you?" he asked.

"No."

As we were talking, Monica and Tez finally came inside of the house

"Asha, why you won't want to give me Monica's number?" he asked.

"Because I told you I didn't want you having my friend out here looking crazy. You a hoe, and nobody has time to be kicking your flings' ass," I said.

"I told you if she said it once, she would say it again," Monica said.

I couldn't do anything but laugh because Kairo was just shaking his head and laughing at me. I didn't care how he felt about it because it was the truth.

"You going to the school tomorrow?" Monica asked.

"Yeah, I have to get my schedule and books and stuff. You want to meet up there?" I asked.

"Yeah. Let's meet there at noon," she said.

"Alright, my G, I'll see you tomorrow," Tez said.

My body was beginning to hurt again, so I knew it was time for me to shower and relax. It had been a busy day. From the time that I woke up, I had been moving all day. Finishing up, I went upstairs to find Kairo lying across the bed in his boxers watching a movie on TV.

"Well, thanks for the help," I said.

"I thought you were finished, my bad, bae," he replied.

I went into that bathroom to start the shower and to wrap my hair. I came back out to see that he was now scrolling on his phone and smoking a blunt.

"Bae, when you think you could take this trip?" he asked.

"It would have to be after I finish the first semester of school," I replied.

"Just let me know when you are getting close to finishing the semester," he said.

Going back into the bathroom and stepping into the shower, I let the warm water run over my body. It soothed my aching body. Lathering up my sponge with my bodywash, I had to take it easy over some of my bruises because they were hurting. When I finished drying off, I went back into the bedroom to find Kairo still watching TV.

"Asha, come lay across the bed," he said, patting the bed.

Walking over to the bed, I laid across the bed with my panties and no bra. I didn't even notice that there was a bottle of oil on the nightstand. Pouring the warm oil on my back, he turned on some music and began to massage my back with his strong hands. No words were spoken between me and him. It was the true definition of intimacy. His hands felt so good against my body that I fell asleep in no time.

When I woke up in the morning, he was sound asleep. He hadn't been sleeping lot since the whole incident with me, Mari, and Justice. He would always fall asleep but would wake up in the middle of the night. It had been times that I would wake up, and he would sit on the balcony smoking a cigar or would just be watching TV from the bed. I tried to slip out of bed without waking him. No sooner than I made it to the bathroom, I heard him wake up and grab his phone.

Using the bathroom to relieve myself, once I was finished, I washed my face and brushed my teeth. As I was finishing up, he walked into the bathroom to relieve himself and freshen up also. Looking at the time, it was about nine o'clock. I had enough time to make breakfast and to go down in the gym to work out a little before it was time for me to head to the school.

Going downstairs, I went ahead and let the dogs out to run in the backyard and started breakfast. When Kairo made his way down to the kitchen, I was just about finished with cooking.

"So I'm going to let you drive today because I have a meeting that I need to get to," he said.

"Oh, no chauffer today?" I asked sarcastically.

"Keep it up, and your ass will be locked in the house fucking with me," he replied.

I fixed his plate while he went out and got the dogs their water and food. I placed his plate on the counter in front of the stool and waited. Coming back in, he washed his hands and poured both of us something to drink. For some reason, my mail still hadn't been sent to the house. I was going to go to the apartment to see if there was any mail in the box.

Sitting down next to Kairo, we began eating our food. No sooner than we put the fork in our mouths, Kairo's phones began to go off.

"What's up?" he said.

He got up and went outside to talk while I finished my food and went down to the gym to run on the treadmill for a little bit. He came downstairs and jumped on the other one for a little bit before telling me that he was going to take a shower so that he could get ready for his meeting. I ran for about twenty more minutes before I came from the basement to get my phone that was on the counter.

While I was coming up the stairs, he was coming down. Stopping in the middle, he told me that he had left some money on my dresser and that he was letting the dogs back into the house. Kissing him goodbye, he headed downstairs while I went up to my room to find something to wear for the day. I was going to text Monica and see if she just wanted me to come and get her since I would be coming that way to check the mail.

Me: Hey, girl. You want me to come and scoop you?

Mo: It's up to you. I don't want you to go out of your way.

Me: I have to come that way anyway to check the mail at the old apartment.

Mo: Well, you can come since you will be over here.

Me: Okay. I will be that way at eleven.

Getting up off the bed, I went into the bathroom to shower again because I was sweaty as hell from running on the treadmill. When I came out of the bathroom, going into the closet, I saw that Kairo had left me a wad of money along with the keys to his truck. I got dressed, grabbed my checkbook, phone, and keys and headed out the door after putting the alarm on. Driving down the highway to Monica's house, I had the sunroof open, and the sun was shining through with the wind blowing through my hair.

When I pulled up to Monica's house, I sent her a text that I was outside, and she told me to come up because she wasn't ready yet. Coming up the stairs, I remembered the days from when she and I would sit on these same exact steps and listen to music in the summertime and watch the boys play football in the street. Knocking on the door, a lady came to the door to open it.

"You must be Asha," the lady said.

"Yes, that would be me."

"Monica has been talking about you. You don't remember me? I'm Monica's aunt Mary," she said.

"Yes, you use to take us skating with your daughter. How is she?" I asked.

"Chile, she somewhere out here strung out on drugs, having baby after baby," she replied.

"Oh, wow! She had a good head on her shoulders also," I stated.

"She still does. She was in school before she met up with that no-good nigga she with now. He sorry as hell and keeps having babies by her but won't claim any of them," she mumbled.

"That's a shame. Where are the children now?" I asked.

"She just had one two days ago that's still in the hospital strung out on crack. I told the doctors that I would take her as soon as they release her. So she could be with her other sister and brother," she sadly said.

"Auntie, what you down here talking about now?" Monica asked.

"I'm just giving Asha the update with your cousin Shondra," she replied.

"Oh, yeah? What about her?" Monica asked.

"I was telling her that she had another baby two days ago and that I'm going to get the baby when they release her," Mary said.

"Aww, what are you going to name her? Do you have anything for her?" I asked.

"I don't know what I'm going to name her, and I'm trying to get her some stuff now," Mary replied.

"I'm going to see what I can get up for the baby and give it to Monica. Let me know when you are going to see her. I would like to visit her also," I said.

I had no idea what the fuck had come over me, but I felt the urge to go see about this baby. The whole situation was sad because Ms. Mary was young by no means, but she still didn't hesitate to take in her grandchildren. Monica and I headed out the door so that we could go and finish up at school so that we could start classes.

When Monica and I got into the car, she was a crazy look on her face.

"Bitch, spill the tea," I said while driving.

"Girl, there is no tea to spill." She blushed.

"Don't lie to me. I know Tez and you were all boo'd up last night before y'all left. You didn't give him none, did you?" I asked.

"Girl, no! You think I'm a hoe or something?" She laughed.

"I'm not saying you're a hoe, but that nigga there has a gift that he could talk the Virgin Mary out of her panties," I replied.

"Not the Virgin Mary!" she screamed.

"I'm serious. He is smooth it too. I saw his ass in action. He is really good people other than that. Just take your time and make that nigga work for it," I said.

As I was driving, Kairo FaceTimed me, so I answered the phone to see what he wanted. I had just pulled up to the old apartment to check the mail. I grabbed my phone and exited the truck.

"What's up, bae?" I asked.

"What you up to?" he asked.

"I stopped by the apartment to check the mail after I picked up Monica. I'm about to head to the school now," I said.

"Ight. Hit me up when you're done so we can meet for lunch," he said.

"Sounds like a plan to me," I said.

As we continued to the school, my mind kept going back to the little baby that was lying in the hospital suffering from the addiction by the hands of her mother. When we pulled into the parking lot of the school, I sat there for a moment before I took the steps to further my education. Getting out of the truck, Monica and I headed into the building to pay our tuition and get the supplies that we needed. After about two hours, Monica and I walked out of the school about ten grand lighter. We had books, bag, uniforms, and anything else that we may need to get us through the first semester of school.

Getting back into the truck, we headed to Kobe's Steakhouse for lunch. I had texted Kairo about fifteen minutes ago, so he should already be there waiting for us. When we arrived at the restaurant, Kairo and Tez were waiting at the table for us. We sat down and waited for the waitress to come and take our orders. Sensing that something was wrong, Kairo stared at me, waiting for me to say something.

"What's the matter with you?" he asked.

"She has been in that funk ever since she talked to my aunt about my baby cousin," Monica said.

"What do you mean?" he asked.

"My aunt was telling her that my cousin has a baby, and she is still in the hospital. She was born addicted to drugs, so until it is completely out of her system and she is okay, she will there," Monica said.

"Thanks a lot, Mo," I said.

"Is that what's wrong?" he asked.

"I don't even know what the matter with me is. It was like when she told me, I just felt sorry for the baby," I said.

Placing our orders, Kairo and Tez asked us how things went at the school. We told them that we had everything set, and we were on schedule to start in two weeks. I was excited and nervous at the same time that I was going back to school. I was glad that Monica was going to be there with me to make it a little easier. While we were eating our food, a chick that was sitting at the next table couldn't take her eyes off Kairo. She looked familiar, but I couldn't remember where I may have seen her. That was until I got a text from Monica telling me that the chick was one of Ameka's friend and that she was there the day of the fight. Thinking that Kairo and Tez weren't paying attention to what Monica and I were doing, Kairo spoke.

"So y'all going to tell us what y'all texting each other about?" he asked.

I looked at him and then to Monica, but before I could say anything, the female approached us.

"Excuse me," she said.

"What's up?" Kairo asked.

"Ummm, I wanted to tell her sorry," she said, looking at me.

"Sorry for what?" he asked, looking at me.

"She was one of the bitches that was there trying to jump Asha. Bet she didn't think that she would run into us again, especially with you," Monica said.

"What the fuck you mean?" Kairo said calmly.

"I didn't know that it was going to go down like that," she whispered.

I could tell that Kairo was trying his best to remain calm as she talked. He was sitting there as Tez as doing something on his phone.

"So where is ole girl?' he asked.

"Who? Ameka?" she questioned.

"No, fucking Big Bird!" He roared.

Causing her to jump, he was now towering over her as he was a whole foot taller than her.

"You have five minutes to tell me what I want to know, or your family will be finding your body parts all over the city!" He snarled.

We were secluded off from the others in the restaurant, so the only ones that could hear what was being said were us.

"I don't know where she went after she dropped off her mother," she insisted.

"Whose mother?" I asked, cutting my eye back at her to see whose mother she was referring to

I knew Kandi and I didn't get along all the time, but I know she didn't hate me that much to damn near kill me.

"Answer her question," Kairo said.

"It was your mother that hit you from behind," she said.

"Look, what's your name?" I asked.

"Dana," she mumbled.

"Dana, if I find out that you're lying when you said that my mother hit me from behind, you won't have to worry about what he is going to do to you because I will kill you my damn self." I threatened.

Grabbing my purse, I left the remainder of my food that was on my plate and took off to the bathroom. I was completely sick to my stomach at the thought that Kandi might've actually tried to hurt me. Everything that I had just eaten came up, along with my breakfast and anything else that I had eaten today. I was hurt and confused all at the same time. Coming out of the bathroom stall, Kairo was sitting on the sink waiting for me.

"Did you know about this?" I asked.

"Indeed," he spoke.

"So when were you going to tell me that my mother tried to kill me by hitting me from behind!" I shouted.

"First thing you are going to do is calm the fuck down with all that yelling and shit. Second, we are going to get in the car and talk about this when we get to the house—it's too many ears," he said.

Washing my hands and drying them, I snatched my purse off the counter and headed straight out of the door, looking for the truck.

"Tez and Mo took the truck. Let's ride," he said, walking to his car.

Getting into the car, I had to be extra and slam the car door just because. The whole ride to the house, I didn't say anything to him. I just kept scrolling through my phone, ignoring him. Pulling into the driveway, I hopped out as soon as the car came to a complete stop. Unlocking the door, I ran straight to the room into the bathroom. I had to vomit again, and I didn't even have anything in my stomach.

Kairo came into the bathroom with a cold ginger ale and placed a cool rag on my neck.

"Ash, you pregnant, ma?" he asked.

"I betta not be. I told you I'm not trying to be a baby momma. I want to be a wife first, and then I can have the children," I announced.

Climbing into the bed, I just wanted to lie down because I wasn't feeling good at all.

"Ash, the reason I didn't tell you about ya moms is that you were already going through it about your sister. I couldn't find the proper words to tell you that your mother had turned against you for someone that she barely knew. How do you find the words to tell someone that?" he questioned.

"Just always keep it a buck with me, whether it will hurt me or not. We won't last with lies and deceit," I said.

"You right. My bad. It won't happen again," he said.

"You coming to lay down with me?" I asked.

"Nah. I have to make a couple calls. Go ahead and rest," he said.

JUSTICE

I damn sure didn't feel like sitting in class today. If it wasn't for Mari making me go, I would've had my ass right in bed still sleeping. My sixth-period class had just ended, and I was waiting on Drea so that we could go to our last class. She was walking down the hallway talking shit to a couple of the football players.

"Girl, why the tea is that your mother was there when your sister got jumped? In fact, she hit her with a stick or something," Drea said.

"Bitch, stop lying. She crazy but not that damn crazy," I stated.

"There is supposed to be some kind of video that has been going around. When I get it, I will send it to you," she said as we entered the classroom.

"I can't believe that my mother would do something like that. I mean, damn... She hates my sister that much?" I said, taking out my phone.

I went to call my mother, but it went straight to voicemail. Sticking my phone into my pocket, I headed into the classroom. The whole time that I was sitting in class, I couldn't focus. My mind was on my mother and what she tried to do to my sister. I loved my sister to death, and the thought of something happening to her... I would die.

The class was over before I knew it, and I don't remember anything that happened or what the teacher even said. My mind was on getting out of this class and heading over to her house to see what the hell was wrong with her. I told Drea that I would take her home since I was heading that way. We walked to the car.

"Girl, that nigga letting you push the whip like that?" she said.

"Yeah. He has to take it easy, so he just gives me the keys to the car to take myself to school," I stated.

We hopped into the car and headed toward Drea's house. I texted Mari to let him know that I was going to my mom's house and to drop off Drea. When I pulled up to the house, Jerry was sitting on the porch smoking a cigarette. Getting out of the truck, he met me halfway up the walkway.

"Have you heard from Kandi?" he asked.

"That's the reason I came over here. I thought she was here. I just heard that she was a part of the crew that jumped Asha," I replied.

"I know. I found out a couple days ago. That woman has some issues. How you turn on your daughter like that?" he asked.

"It's crazy. I knew she felt some kind of way about her, but she crossed the line with this one," I said sadly.

"I know. I'm trying to wait on her because I'm about to go to this program, and I won't be back for a good six months. I was hoping that I would be able to convince her to come, but she hasn't come home," he confessed.

"That is so good for you, Jerry! Don't let Kandi not being here stop you. Go ahead and take care of yourself," I stated.

Getting back into the car, I needed to talk to my sister. Calling Asha, she answered her phone.

"What's up, sis?" she asked.

"I just came from Kandi's house. She isn't here, and Jerry hasn't seen her since the fight."

"I knew that she wouldn't go back there because that would be too easy to find her."

"I'm sorry, sis. I don't know why she treats you like that," I said.

"What you sorry for? Those are her demons that will beat her ass in the end. If I don't ever see her again, it will be perfectly fine with me," Asha said.

It's sad to say that I couldn't blame her though. Asha had tried to have a relationship with our mother. Everything was always fine when she could get what she needed out of my sister, but as soon as she told our mother no, it's like she didn't even know who she was at the time. I knew it hurt my sister plenty of times because she kept trying. I think that it had a lot to do with my grandmother. She always told us to respect our parents, no matter how pissed off they made us.

We finished our conversation as I was pulling up to the condo. I sat in the car for a couple minutes, trying to get my emotions together because they were everywhere, and I didn't want Mari to see me stressed or crying. When I walked into the house, Mari was sitting on the couch watching TV.

"Justice, what's the matter?" he asked, jumping off the couch.

"Nothing. I was just thinking how fucked up things are," I replied.

"What you mean?" he questioned.

"What kind of mother jumps their own child? Someone that they brought into the world?"

Before I knew it, the tears were falling, and I was sobbing into Mari's chest. I had been holding in so much that I had finally had enough. Walking me to the couch, he sat me down so I was now lying on his lap bawling away. I cried so much that I fell asleep right there on his lap.

When I woke up, Mari was in the kitchen talking to someone about a fitting for something. I couldn't make out everything that he was staying because he started talking in codes when she noticed that I was awake. Walking back into the living room, he sat down and put his feet up.

"Mari, what was that about?" I asked.

"Damn, nosy, touch your nose," he replied, laughing.

"So you not going to tell me?" I questioned.

"Let's go out for dinner. What do you have a taste for?" he asked, changing the subject.

"I don't know. You pick," I said, walking off to the room while pouting.

I had been wrapped in my feelings today and just couldn't figure out why. I ran me a tub of water to relax and regroup. It was so much going on lately that I hadn't a chance to just breathe and take it all in. I still hadn't heard anything from the school that I had applied for, and I hadn't finished my project that was due in my anatomy class.

"Justice, where you at, baby?" Mari yelled.

"What's the matter?" I asked.

"You okay?" he asked.

"Yeah. I'm just stressing waiting to hear back from these schools," I said.

"Get dressed. We are taking a ride," he said, leaving out the bathroom.

Drying myself off, I grabbed a pair of PINK tights with a shirt to match and some slides. I unwrapped my hair and met Mari out in the living room. He was wearing a black-and-white Jordan outfit with the slides to make.

"You ready?" he asked while checking his phone.

"Yeah, but where are we going?" I questioned.

"Just ride. Let's go," he ordered, holding the door open.

As we made our way to the garage, Drea called me. Sending her to voicemail, I jumped into the passenger side of the money-green Range Rover. Lighting a blunt, Mari pulled out the garage with the sunroof open and bumped Ball Greezy. The night air was refreshing as the smell of the weed invaded my nostrils. Jumping on the interstate, Mari received a call. It was Aunt Ro.

"Hey, baby. What y'all doing?" she asked.

"I'm taking Jus for a ride. She in her feelings and need to clear her pretty head," he stated with a wink.

"Tell my baby everything will be fine and stop stressing. I'll talk to y'all later. Enjoy the night," she said and hung up.

We drove for about twenty more minutes until we were almost out in the suburbs. Pulling into a parking lot, there was a fair in the mall parking lot with rides, petting zoo, and most of all, fast food.

"I haven't been to one of these in forever," I said.

"That makes two of us then. Let's go," he replied.

We got to the gate, and Mari paid for us to have an armband so that we could ride anything that we wanted. I had my mind set on trying all the deep-fried foods. This was definitely what I needed to take my mind off the stress and drama that had been going on today. I was thankful that Mari was here to take me out of the little pity party that I was trying to have with myself.

We rode on damn near every ride, and Mari spent I'm not sure how much money trying to win all the teddy bears for Blessing and me. I tried all the carnival food, deep-fried Oreos, burgers with donuts, and anything else I could think of. We stayed there for almost five hours, and I had a blast. Everything that I was feeling went on the back burner, and I realized that I couldn't control the things that happened in my life.

When we finally made it home, I was completely exhausted and just wanted to lie down, but I still had to finish homework first. Mari went into the room, leaving me in the living room to do my work. I didn't even remember falling asleep. The next thing I knew, Mari was lifting me up and carrying me to the room, where he took off my clothes and pulled the covers up.

MARI

This shit with Asha and her so-called mother was fucking with my baby bad. I never saw her stressed and down. It was bad enough that she was stressing about getting accepted into these medical programs. I took her to the fair, hoping that I would take her mind off things because she had the look of defeat all over her.

I was glad that she was able to let her hair down for a while at least. No sooner than we made it back to the house, she went right into the books and started studying. I was glad she was getting back into her groove with school. It was important that she went back to her normal routine because I didn't want to stop her at anything that she wanted to accomplish. I wasn't sure if she wanted to go back to work, but if she didn't want to, that was fine with me.

I hadn't heard from Kendra since the day at the park when she showed her ass. Something told me to stay home and not go, but me trying to be the nice one backfired on me. Kairo told me a long time ago about her, and

I wished that I'd listened. Maybe I wouldn't have a baby with a chick that I couldn't stand to look at, let alone even like. A couple minutes of pleasure turned into a bunch of bullshit for no fucking reason.

Lying in the bed, I watched as Justice slept. I had a habit of waking up and watching her while she slept. My phone went off. I tried to silence it before Justice woke up. Answering the phone, it was Kairo calling me.

"What's up?" I whispered.

"Nigga, what you whispering for?" he asked.

"What the hell you calling so damn early for? You know people do sleep, unlike your Dracula ass." I joked.

"That's when I do my best thinking," he said.

"Yeah, okay. What's up?" I questioned.

"I want you to come through the house later today. I need to talk to you about something," he said.

"Nigga, you couldn't text me that shit?" I said.

"I wanted you to hear me when I said that." He laughed, hanging up.

Hanging up the phone, I tried to get comfortable so that I could sleep before it was time for Justice to wake. No sooner than I closed my eyes, Justice's alarm went off, indicating it was time for her to wake up. I was going to take her to school today because I had plans for her after school. She didn't know it, but I was planning to take her to a dressmaker to get her prom dress custom made. I wanted to make this a night that she wouldn't forget.

"Justice, get up so you won't be late," I said.

"I don't feel like going today," she whined.

"Come on, Jus. We don't have that much longer, so push through the final weeks, and you'll be done," I replied.

Getting out of the bed, she walked to the shower and started the water. While she was doing that, I went and made me a cup of coffee and sat and watched TV. Once I dropped her off, I was going over to Robi's house so that I could check on Blessing. As I was sitting, watching TV, I heard Justice screaming in the room. Jumping up, I headed to the room to see what she was screaming about.

Walking in, she was standing naked and dancing to herself. Completely puzzled, I stood there waiting for her to tell me what was going on.

"Bae, look!" she said, showing me her phone.

Looking at her phone, I looked at the email that she was showing me. Reading the email that was addressed to her, it stated that she was accepted to UPenn in their medical program.

"Oh, shit, bae! Congratulations!" I said.

"Yes. That is the one I really wanted too," she said, turning to get dressed.

My bae was on cloud nine. It looked like she was floating on air since she got the news of her acceptance. As we pulled up to the school, she sat there for a minute before getting out.

"What?" I asked.

"I just can't believe that I got accepted into the school," she said, smiling.

"It will only go up from here love," I said, leaning over and kissing her.

As I was pulling away, I saw her walk up to a friend, and they both started hugging and bouncing in the air. On my way to Robi's house, I called to make sure she that she didn't need anything before I got there. She told me to stop and grab Blessing some more diapers and wipes on my way in. Pulling into Walmart, it was already busy. I swear, I hated coming into this place. The combination of old ass people pushing carts and the crazy ass chick whose American Express card were loaded with carts full of food.

Grabbing a cart, I headed straight to the baby section and loaded the cart with diapers and wipes so that she would be set for a while. I made sure to grab a couple boxes so that I could take them to my house also. Checking out in the express lane, the customer service chick couldn't take her eyes off me long enough to help the customer she was helping. She even went so far as to drop something near the register that I was checking out on so that she could bend over to try to show me her flat ass butt.

"You can save it, ma. I'm damn near married." I laughed.

"Boy, ain't no one worried about you," she snapped.

"Yeah, that's what you say now, but your body language says otherwise," I replied, grabbing my receipt and walking off.

By the time that I made it to Robi's house, Kairo was there also. Getting out of the truck, I grabbed as many boxes that I could and headed into the house. Kairo was sitting at the table with Blessing in his arms, feeding her whatever he was eating. I was glad that he was here; I would be able to kill two birds with one stone and get whatever he wanted to talk to me about over with.

"I'm glad that your ass is here. We can talk about whatever you wanted to talk about," I said, setting down the diapers and walking back out the door.

As I was walking back into the house, my phone rang, and it was the dress designer.

"Hello, Kamari. This Renee, Stella's assistant. I was calling to confirm your appointment for this afternoon at three p.m.," she said.

"Yes. We are on for three p.m. I should be arriving a little early about 2:30-2:45. Is that okay?" I replied.

"That will be a good time. It will give us time for her to look at some of the designs that she must like," she replied.

"Okay, we will see you then," I said, hanging up.

Hanging up the phone, I walked back into the house, taking everything that I had brought Blessing upstairs to her room. Once I finished, I sat down at the table where Robi had a plate ready for me. She sat down with us, and we all ate quietly while Blessing blew spit bubbles at us.

"Justice got accepted to UPenn this morning," I said.

"That's what's up. I'm proud of her. I knew she could do it," Kairo said.

"Miya got accepted to the same school too. What if they decided to go to the same school?" Robi said.

"It would be easier on all of us. We wouldn't have to worry, and they could look out for one another," Kairo said.

"Yeah, that would work. I probably would get them a house or something up there so they could get away from the dorm on the weekends," I said.

"True, let me know what she decides. Maybe we could get them both on the same page and see if it would work," Kairo said.

"So what is it you want to talk to me about, big bro?" I asked.

"So we going to hit those niggas in two days. I know that you have a child that you have to be here for. So with that being said, I'm sitting you out for this ride. I don't want to hear shit about it. I thought long and hard about this. I damn near lost you a minute ago, so I won't take any chances," he said.

I was mad as hell that he didn't want me to come along, but I understood where he was coming from.

"I feel you, bro. Asha got a nigga acting all soft and shit." I laughed.

"Nawl, it was just a real moment for me when I got the call that day that your car was shot up," he replied.

"I'm taking Justice later today to get her prom dressed designed. I'm going all out for my baby," I said.

"That's good, bro. How is she holding up?" he asked.

"She hurt like shit when she found out that her moms had something to do with Asha getting jumped and landing in the hospital," I said.

"Yeah, Asha was in her feelings a lil' bit too," Kairo said.

"Her mother isn't shit for that, and she better not let me see her because I'm going to kick her ass for the old and the new!" Robi yelled from the kitchen.

"Well, damn, I thought you took Blessing upstairs," Kairo said.

"You know I move in silence," she responded.

I had to laugh because Robi over here thinking that she was a gangsta. Getting up, I ran up the stairs to check on Blessing. She was lying there playing with her feet and looking at the animals on the baby mobile hanging over her bed. Picking her up and setting her down in the rocking chair, I turned on the TV to her favorite cartoon.

She watched it for about five minutes, and she was knocked out sleep. As I was lying her back down in her bed, I noticed that both Kairo and Robi were looking at the both of us. Walking past the both them, I walked down the stairs into the living room.

"That's why her ass is spoiled now," Robi said.

"Yep. Just like Miya, so what's the problem?" I said.

"Y'all did that, not me. I think Blessing might be worst because everyone spoils her," she replied.

"Look, I'm about to head out. I have a couple moves I need to make. Bro, hit me up, and let me know how the appointment went," Kairo said.

"What appointment?" Robi asked.

"I'm taking Justice to get a custom prom dress made," I replied.

I stayed at Robi's house until it was just about time for me to go and pick up Justice. Blessing woke up about thirty minutes –after I laid her down, so I spent most of my time with her while Robi ran her errands. When she finally made it back to the house, I told her that I would be back after the appointment so she could spend a couple days with me at the house.

BUDAH

I was proud of the man that my brother was becoming. Him having Blessing calmed him down a little. I watched as he sat and rocked Blessing to sleep in the nursery and wondered if I would be the same type of father. Shaking that off, I pulled up the warehouse. Tez, Midnight, Taj, and Kiah was waiting for me. We had finally got confirmation that Tyshawn was working with the state. From what Tez friend said, there wasn't a lot of information that they had because it was just starting, but the damage had already been done, and he now had to pay for running his mouth.

When I walked into the warehouse, everyone was standing around talking and sipping on Coronas.

"What's y'all niggas doing?" I asked.

"We are waiting for you to get here so we can get this shit over with," Taj said.

Walking past them, I went downstairs to the bunker that I had made for cases like this. Tyshawn was sitting there blindfolded with no clothes on. It was because of me that he was able to wear those clothes. The same way that he was brought into this world was going to be the same way that he left out of it, naked.

Tez took the blindfold off Tyshawn, and imagine the look on his face when he saw us in the room. It was right there at the moment he knew that he fucked with the wrong one.

"Hey, Budah. What's this about?" he asked.

"Please don't insult my intelligence and act like you don't know what this is about," I said.

"I don't, man. Please fill me in," he said nervously.

"Seems you are suffering from memory loss, so let me refresh it for you. I confirmed with multiple people that you have been working with the state against us," I said.

"Nawl, I wouldn't do you like that," he said.

"Oh, you wouldn't? I figured you would say something like that, so I want you to listen to something and tell does the voice sound familiar," I said.

Signaling for Kiah to play the recording that he had gotten ahold of. It was his voice telling the detectives where the stash house was and what day would be better to hit it. When he realized that we had a tape with his voice on it, his whole posture changed in the chair.

"Look, man, I'm sorry. They pressured me to give them information on who was pushing weight over in that area," he said.

"Nigga, is that supposed to be some kind of justification for you giving up information on an organization that supplied you with money and food for your family on a daily basis?" I said.

"We treated you like family, and this is how you repay the man that took care of your seeds when you couldn't?" Tez hissed.

"I know... I'm sorry, man. The little chick that I was messing with turned out to be seventeen, and her peoples found out and pressed charges against me," he said.

"That still doesn't justify you turning on us. Nigga, we would've handled that and had your back," I replied.

I still was having trouble with this lame ass excuse that he was trying to give about some lil' chick he was messing with. Something was strange about that because we never saw him look at any chick or have them around. Pulling Midnight to the side, I told him to have Mills run his phone records because his story seemed shaky to me.

I was completely done with the whole situation. Walking away, I gave my man Lang the signal to do what he did best. No sooner than I got up the stairs, I could hear the screams and pleads coming from Tyshawn. Turning the music on so that I wouldn't hear anything, I sat at my desk and scrolled through my phone.

Everyone filtered in the office one by one as we waited for Lang to finish cutting up the body into small pieces. I was going to have his body spread over the city to be pieced together, since he wanted to give out information on my business. This would be an unsolved murder because nothing would be recognizable.

"Man, damn, he ain't finished yet?" Kiah asked.

"Nawl. Lang is a mastermind with this shit," I replied.

"What we finna eat? I'm hungry as hell," Taj asked.

We all jumped into our cars and headed to grab something to eat. I needed to talk about the hit that was about to take place. We were seated in a private dining area so that others couldn't hear. We all talked in codes, which we only knew.

We agreed that we would do a five-day strike, taking out any and everything that was in our way. We were trying to draw out the nigga Nasir, since he was the boss. I wanted to see if he was about that action when the pressure was on. I was going to have everyone out of the city so they couldn't be touched or found for the next five days. I had a cabin way out in a secluded area that only a few of us knew about.

Me: Bae, I need you to pack a bag for about a week.

Wife: Okay. Where we going?

Me: We aren't going anywhere. I need you and the family safe for a min.

Wife: Okay, you are scaring me. Is everything okay?

Me: Yeah. Shit about to get crazy, and I need to make sure that everyone that I love is safe so I can do what I need to do

Wife: When are we leaving?

Me: Tomorrow night.

Wife: K.

I knew that Asha was confused about what I just texted her. Once I got face-to-face, I would explain to her what was about to take place. I had a bank account setup in her name with my banking info, and it had roughly ninety grand in it. I was going to give her the information on that, along with where to find my safe-deposit keys and other business papers. I was going to give her instructions to give them to Robi, in case of emergency.

"Tez, are you sending Monica and her people with the rest of the family?" I asked.

"Do you think that I should?" he asked.

"If you want them safe, I suggest that you send them. We can't have any fuckups because niggas' minds are elsewhere, instead of what they are doing at that moment," I stated.

"I feel you. I'm going to text her to pack up her family and to make sure that her mother has enough meds," he said.

"If she can't get them all, let me know. I'll hire her a nurse that can be with her for the time being with security," I replied.

"Y'all got everything taken care of in here?" Midnight asked.

"Yeah. I just finished working out the details with Asha. I'll call Robi and Mari in a min and tell them what the move is," I informed.

As I was sitting back waiting on my food to arrive, my mind went wondering again on the life that I was living and what it would feel like to be behind the scenes and just enjoy life. I watched my brothers Taj and Midnight do it with such ease. I wondered if I would be able to pull it off also. I wasn't quite ready, because I wanted to make sure that I had the right people in place, but that was the ultimate goal.

"What you over here thinking about?" Taj asked.

"Thinking about what life would be outside of the game," I replied.

"Nigga, life is gucci. Don't have to worry about the bullshit. Just enjoy life, especially when niggas think that you really out, ya feel me."

"I'm thinking long and hard about it. I'm getting older,

and it's time to slow down and enjoy the fruit of my labor."

"I can definitely understand that. Get you a loyal ass team that will hold the business down faithfully and just stay in the cut and monitor. That is how Night and I did it, and we're still doing it. A lot of people just believe that we are in real estate, and that is just how we like it," he responded.

"Yeah, I'm going to start getting my feet wet in a couple businesses to make some legal money also."

"Let me know if you need help," he stated and got up from the table.

When we arrived back at the warehouse, Lang was coming up the stairs as if nothing had happened.

"We good?" I asked.

"Yeah. You can call the cleanup crew," he replied.

Tez took out his phone and called the funeral home that we used when we needed to get rid of something without anyone knowing. We were going to have the crew clean the parts up and take it to them so that they could burn the body. The cleanup crew was professional, if that's what you wanted to call it. They owner had experience from working in the morgue, so he knew all the products to use to make sure that there weren't any traces of blood and fluids.

I left Tez to make sure that everything was taken care of, telling him that I would see him and the rest of the guys tomorrow. I had to make a couple stops—one to Robi's house, and the other would be to Mari's house, once he returned from surprising Justice. I called Asha to see where she was. She was just making her way into the house. Pulling into the driveway, I left the car running while I ran in the house to use the bathroom and tell Asha to ride with me.

I hadn't noticed that she was sitting in the living room when I came out of the bathroom. She was just sitting there like she had been told the worst news in the world.

"Hey, what's the matter?" I asked.

She still had her phone in her hand, so she might've just got off it.

"That was the police calling to tell me that they found Kandi's body in an abandoned building that caught on fire," she whispered.

"Wait, what?" I interrupted.

"Yeah, they said they she was dead before the fire even started. It was a known squatter house," she added.

"Woah, are you alright? I mean, she did some fucked-up shit, but she still was ya moms," - replied.

"I'm fine. I just can't believe that she is gone. I mean, my mother technically died years ago though," she proclaimed.

"Are you going to tell Justice?" I asked.

"Yeah, I'm going to call her in a minute," she replied.

"Wait, her and Mari went to see the dress designer for her custom dress for prom. Don't mess up this moment for her," I pleaded.

"You're right. I won't spoil her moment. What you about to do?" she asked.

"Come take a ride to Robi's house with me."

Locking up the house, we jumped into the car and headed to Robi's house. It was fucked up the way that Kandi went out. I wonder who was responsible for burning her though. That damn sure wasn't my doing. I watched as Asha stared off into space as we drove over to Robi's house. I texted Mari to bring Justice over to the house when they were done. I wanted to give him the play, and we also had to break the news to Justice about Kandi.

ASHA

After all the drama that Kandi and I had been through, I would never wish her ending on my worst nightmare. I guess the way that you lived was the way that you went out. I knew that I was wrong for feeling the way that I was feeling, but ever since my grandma Dot passed, life with her was a complete nightmare, not to mention that she went against her own daughter for some chick that had a beef with me.

I was sitting in Kairo's truck trying to figure out how I was going to tell Justice that Kandi was dead. I knew that she was going to be devasted because she would always try to see the better side of her. The police wanted me to come and claim the body whenever I had a moment. I told them that I was about to leave for a couple days and would when I returned.

The car pulled into Robi's driveway. I hadn't even noticed that we were here. I was so busy thinking about what the next step with the Kandi situation would be. I didn't even hear a word that Kairo said or if he even said anything to me.

Opening the car door so that I could get out, Kairo looked into my eyes when he spoke to me.

"I need you to talk to me about what you are feeling and thinking. I can't help you if I don't know what is going on," he said.

Kissing me on the forehead, he moved out of the way so that I could go into the house with him hot on my trail. Walking into the house, I walked right up to Robi and broke down crying. I didn't even know it was happening until I saw her.

"OMG, Kairo! What did you do to her?" Robi asked.

"Robi, I swear to God I didn't do anything to her. She just found out that Kandi is dead," he explained.

"My Lord! Baby, come on in here and sit down," Robi said.

I was so filled with hurt, anger, sorrow, and anguish that my emotions took over me. Here I was crying my eyes out about a woman who didn't like, love, and probably wished I was dead at times, like she was the best mother in the world.

"Kairo, come hold her. I have to take my pot off the stove," she said.

Standing over me, he scooped me up in his arms and sat down so that I was now sitting on his lap, laying my head on his shoulder as I continued to cry.

"Asha, you're going to be okay, bae. I got you," he said.

As he was saying this, Mari and Justice walked into the house. I could hear the excitement in her voice when she walked in.

"I can't wait to tell Ash. Where she at?" she asked.

"I'm right here, Jus," I responded.

Coming into the living room where we were, Kairo was placing me beside him so that I could talk to her.

"What's the matter, Ash?" Justice asked.

"I'm okay. Where you been?" I asked.

"I just came from a fitting for my prom dress that Mari is getting custom made for me," she said with a grin.

"Oh my God! Justice, that is exciting! Did you get everything picked out?" I asked.

"Yes, I gave her the vision I had in my head, and she went from there. This dress is going to be lit," she said.

I watched as my sister described her dress and the fabric of the dress, and there was no way that I could give her the news about Kandi. Deciding that I would want until tomorrow to let her know what happened, she continued telling me that she had finally been accepted to her top choice, UPenn, for their medical program.

While we were talking, Kairo and Mari went off to talk on the back porch in private. As they were talking, Miya came in and told us that she had been accepted to UPenn and John Hopkins. This was exciting news for the both of them. The sad information that I had received would have to go to the backburner while we celebrated the girls getting accepted into college.

Robi had already started cooking, so she had to finish up, and then we could eat. Miya's little friend, along with Monica and Tez, joined us for dinner. Robi had cooked enough to feed an army. Of course, Kairo, Tez, and Mari ate like they hadn't been fed in years while we all looked at them like they were crazy.

Once they finished, they went back out to the patio to talk of course. We cleared the table and started cleaning up with Robi so it wouldn't be all on her once everyone left. Once they came back into the house, they asked Miya to walk Javon to the door because it was time to discuss family business. Doing as she was told, she walked him to the front porch where they said their goodnights.

We were all in the kitchen cleaning when Kairo started talking.

"So I wanted everyone here to pack a bag for the next week. It's some stuff that's about to go on in the next few days, and I don't want any of my loved ones around when the drama starts. I need to be able to focus on the task, and I can't do that with me not knowing where everyone is. Mari will be going with you, and I will be sending Biggs and someone else also," he stated.

"Wait, where are we going?" Miya asked.

"To an undisclosed location. There will be food, water, and electricity, but all cellphones, laptops, and electronics will be given to Mari prior to leaving."

"Well, damn, is this a G-14 classified mission or something?" Robi joked.

Kairo cut his eyes at her to let her know that now wasn't the time to be joking and playing around with him. "Everyone is to meet here tomorrow at six p.m., and we will take you to the location," he said.

I turned to Monica because I knew that she had her daughter and mother that she was probably worried about.

"Monica, I'm going to have a nurse to come be with your mother while you are gone. Don't worry. She will be in good hands. I had them checked out, and they are straight. Your daughter, on the other hand, can come with you," he stated.

"Well, I guess we all need to start packing for tomorrow," Robi said.

Everyone began gathering their things so that they could leave and get things ready for tomorrow. Kairo and I got into the car. I was completely silent because I didn't know what to say at the moment. As we were driving, I noticed that he kept looking at me from the corner of my eye.

"Asha, what is the matter?" he asked.

"Kairo, what is going on?" I asked.

"Baby, the less I tell you, the better. If something happens to me, I want you to be telling the truth when you say you don't know anything,"

When he said that, it completely scared the shit out of me.

"What do you mean if something happens?" I asked.

Pulling over in a parking lot, he put the car in park and turned to car off. Turning to look me in the eyes, he took a deep breath before speaking.

"Baby, what's about to go on is dangerous, and there is a possibility that I may not come home to you. Naturally, the goal is to make it back and move on with life, but sometimes, that's just not in the cards," he stated.

Starting the car back up, we continued the drive to the house. My mind went from the situation at hand back to Kandi. My phone rang, snapping me out of my thoughts.

"Hello."

"Asha, this is Ms. Mary. I was calling because you asked me to call you when I was going back to visit the baby. I'm going up there tomorrow about nine o'clock," she said.

"Okay, I'll come up there to see her," I replied.

"OK, baby. I will see you tomorrow. Enjoy the rest of your evening," she said, hanging up.

"Who was that?" Kairo asked.

"That was Monica's aunt Mary. She was calling to let me know that she was going to see the baby in the morning."

"What is it with you and this baby?" he asked.

"I'm not sure. It's something about a baby being brought into the world being addicted to drugs," I said.

"I understand where you're coming from, baby," Kairo said.

As we entered the house, I walked straight to the kitchen to let Simba and Nyla out to relieve themselves. Pouring me a glass of water, Kairo walked up behind me, kissing on the nape of my neck and sucking on my ear lifting me up and placing me on the cold, marble countertops. Ripping a hole into the tights that I was wearing, he entered one finger inside of me. I was already soaking wet before he set me on the counter.

"Damn, you soaking, baby," he said.

Unbuckling his pants and releasing his manhood, he entered inside of me. I sucked in the air as I adjusted to him. Thrusting his hips inside and out, I laid back on the cool counter. Tearing the shirt that I was wearing so that my bra was showing, he fondled my breasts through the lace fabric. I lifted so that I could unbuckle it. Releasing my breasts, I began to caress my breasts as his manhood crashed inside of my canal.

Lifting me up, he walked us over to the dining room-chair where he sat down and allowed me to ride him.

"Ride this dick, baby," he said.

As he was sucking on my breasts, I continued to grind my hips until I couldn't talk it any longer.

"I got to cum," I said, almost out of breath.

"Let that shit go, baby," he said.

We released at the same time and rested against the chair, trying to catch our breath. Easing myself off him, I had to laugh. I was standing there with shreds of clothes that he had ripped off me.

"What's so funny?" he asked.

"You could've just told me to take off my clothes," I said.

Making our way up to the bedroom so that I could shower, Kairo retreated to his favorite spot in the house to smoke his cigar. When I was finished in the bathroom and returned to the room, there was a piece of luggage lying on the bed waiting for me. While I was in the closet getting some of my things, Kairo went and took his shower. I was trying my best to be strong, but on the inside, I was a complete basket case. Here I was falling for a man that may not even make it to the future because of the life he lived.

Shaking off the thoughts that were going through my head, I continued to pack my things. Kairo returned from out of the bathroom and went into his closet, where he came back with a folder.

"Bae, sit down for a minute," he said.

As I was sitting down, he was pulling up a chair close to me.

"Here is the information for the accounts that are in

your name. One of them is a business account, and there will be a monthly deposit into that account in the event that I don't make it back to you. This is the information for the lawyers. He will know exactly what to do if you have to call him. There is also money in an account for Justice and your school also," he stated.

"I don't want to think about you not making it back to me," I said with tears falling down my cheek.

"Look, this is all just in case. I have every intention of making it back, but if something happens, I need to make sure everything is taken care of ahead of time," he replied.

Still sobbing to myself, Kairo went to let the dogs back in the house. We had been so into each other that we completely forgot about them being outside. By the time that he had made it back upstairs, I was completely over packing and had the suitcase on the floor, and I was now watching TV.

"Done packing?" he asked.

"For now, I'll finish when I wake up in the morning. My head is hurting," I replied.

"Do you want me to go with you tomorrow to see this baby?" he asked.

"If you would like to. I'm not forcing you or anything like that," I replied.

"Yeah, I'll go with you. I don't have anything planned in the morning," he said.

Getting into the bed with me, we flicked the channel until we found something that we both agreed on and ended up falling asleep before the first commercial.

MARI

I knew that Justice was going to be crushed when Asha told her about Kandi. Even though she was mad at her at the moment, she still cared for her. I was watching Justice pack our things. I think that I was more worried about her reaction than my brothers going out there in the street to deal with the nigga and his crew.

"What are you staring at?" Justice asked.

"Nothing. I was just thinking about how you looked when we pulled up to the dress designer's shop," I replied.

"OMG! You did really good with that one. I would've never thought that was what we were doing. I thought you were shopping for clothes or something." She giggled.

"I was glad that I was able to put a smile on your face," I replied.

"Baby, what is going on? Why does Kairo want us away for a while?" she asked.

"Bae, it's best that you don't know what is going on.

He knows what he is doing; otherwise, I would be in full disagreement with it," I said.

"Well, at least we all will be together under one roof," she stated.

It was killing me not to be able to tell her what was going on with her mother, but I wanted to make sure that her sister was the one to tell her that. I went downstairs to the safe in my weight room to make sure I packed all the equipment that I needed. I had every kind of weapon that you could think of—some legal and some illegal. Making sure that I had everything that I needed, I returned to the room to find Justice sitting there watching the news.

There was a story about a woman's body being found in an abandoned house that caught on fire. It was saying that the body was badly burnt with no identification on them.

"Damn, that is a messed-up way to go out," Justice said.

"Yeah, that's pretty fucked up," I replied.

As I was about to jump in the shower, I received a call from none other than Kendra's ass. I wondered what the hell she wanted. I damn sure wasn't bringing Blessing to see her anytime soon after the way she showed her ass.

"What is it, Kendra?" I asked.

"Hey. I was wondering if I could get some money from you. We about to be put out on the street if we don't pay the landlord," she replied.

"See? What I tell you about biting the hand that feeds you," I said into the speakerphone.

"I bet if your little girlfriend asked you for the money, you would give it to her," she replied.

"There you go worrying about shit that you have no

business worrying about. But you're right... my lady can get anything that she wants from me."

"Why do you have to be an asshole all the time, Kamari? I didn't ask to get pregnant by you, and I damn sure didn't ask for you to take my baby away from me!" she yelled.

"That's where you fucked up. When I gave you the band to terminate the pregnancy, you wanted to be a spiteful bitch and go shopping and fuck up the money. What kind of father would I be if I let my daughter stay in a house with motherfuckers that are unfit to care for her? You bitches won't kill my baby with y'all careless asses!" I snarled.

"Blessing was fine here with us," her dumb ass said.

"Look, I'm not about to argue with you. I don't have shit for you. My daughter does not lay her head there, so I don't owe you shit. Get the fuck off my line with the bullshit," I said, hanging the phone up.

"Well, she has some nerve," Justice said.

"I know! She better call the nigga that she's messing with because this bank is closed."

Going back to what I was doing, I headed to the bathroom to turn the water on. My phone rang again. This time, it was Blaze calling. She was telling me that some man had come looking for Tyshawn and asked had I heard from him. After telling her that I hadn't seen or heard from him in a lil' minute, after I hung up the phone, I headed to the bathroom. This time, I entered the shower.

I knew what happened to the nigga, but it wasn't my place to tell Blaze what happened to him. If she really wanted to know, she knew who to ask. I wasn't calling the shots, but if it was up to me, all the crew captains would've witnessed what happened when they ran their mouth. I knew Kairo though. He was going to be on some sneaky, serial-killer type shit. Then the whole time acting concerned with the family, offering to take care of the services. You know shit like that to make himself look like the good guy. I got to say he learned from Midnight. Those two right there were crazy as hell when it came to people that being disloyal.

When I finally got out of the shower, Justice was in the bed with her glasses on reading a book. Justice didn't know it, but I had so many surprises for her over the next few months. I was proud of my baby. She had been having a hard time, and she had taken everything that had come her way head-on.

She was sitting there with her glasses on and some boy shorts. I had been trying my best to contain myself with her. Lord knows I got the blue balls because I was in need of something warm, tight, and wet. I didn't want just anyone though. I wanted her. She had been saving herself for the right person. I just wanted to live up to the standards that she had set for the man to take her precious jewel.

When I came to bed, she put her book down and took off her glasses and laid on my chest and watched TV until she dozed off sleep. I didn't mind. It was something completely different from what I used to, but sometimes, change was a good thing. Turning off the light in the room, I laid there and listened to Justice lightly snore on my chest as I watched Netflix and eventually fell asleep myself.

When I woke up the next morning, there was bacon

frying. I threw on some basketball shorts and headed down the stairs to see that Justice was standing in the kitchen with her headphones on, dancing with her back to me. She had some moves too. She had to be dancing to some ass shaking music because she was throwing it around like she was about to break her back.

I had to sit at the island for a good five to eight minutes as she turned over the bacon, cracked eggs, and stirred the potatoes that were on the stove. When she finally turned around, she damn near dropped the pan that she had in her hand.

"Boy! Don't sneak up on me like that!" she yelled.

"You were feeling that song, wasn't you?" I laughed.

Throwing the towel at me, she began to laugh also. Opening the refrigerator, she grabbed the orange juice and poured me a glass.

"I'm starving, so I cooked a little bit of everything, so I have bacon, sausage, eggs, cheese grits, ham, and French toast," she said.

"Well, damn. Who all are you trying to feed? The neighbors?" I asked.

"I told you that I was hungry."

As she was fixing our plates, Kairo called me, telling me that he and Asha were coming over after they leave the hospital. We were just about to sit down when Robi, Miya, and Blessing knocked on the door.

"Damn, it smells good as hell in here," Robi said.

"That's my baby. She cooked a shit load of it too," I replied.

"Justice, you cooked all this food, girl?" Miya asked.

"Yeah. When I get stressed, I cook. On top of that, I was hungry also," she replied.

"Girl, I'm gonna have to put your butt in the kitchen. This food good as hell," Robi said, stuffing a fork in her mouth.

"Robi, why in the hell are you up and moving around this early out and about, like you haven't slept at all?" I asked.

"Well, I had to get up to get some food for this getaway that we are going on. I don't know where we are going, but I wanted to be sure that we had all of the things I could think of to cook and keep my mind off worrying," she replied.

That was something that I just noticed that she and Justice had in common. When they are stressed, they either cooked or cleaned. Justice hadn't mastered the art of shopping yet, but hanging around Miya, she would soon pick that up.

Putting Blessing in her bouncy that was hanging on the door frame, I sat down to eat while Justice, my sis, and Robi sat at the counter and talked. The next thing I knew, Kairo and Asha were coming through the door.

"Damn, Robi, you got this kitchen going on this morning," Asha said.

"That's all Justice's doing," Robi replied.

I knew that dark cloud was about to hang over my baby's head as soon as I watched Asha's mood change as she ate and talked to everyone. When she was finished, she went into the kitchen and started cleaning. I was trying to figure out what was with these women. They were either cooking or cleaning when they become stressed. Once she finished, she asked Justice to come sit with her in the living room, where Kairo and I were seated.

JUSTICE

I thought Asha had a surprise for me because everyone was sitting around looking crazy, but when she asked for me to come and sit down, I knew something was up. The whole time that we sat there, she wouldn't look at me. She stared down at her hands. Taking a deep breath, she began to speak.

"Justice, Kandi is dead. She was found burned badly in that house fire that has been on the news," she stated.

As she was speaking, I completely zoned out. In the back of my mind, I was thinking that this was a dream and that she was going to say she was playing at any moment. When she finally looked up at me, she had tears rolling down her face.

"Are you serious?" I asked.

"Yes, I found out yesterday, but you were so happy about your fitting with the dress designer. I decided to tell you today instead," she replied.

"Do they know who is responsible for the house fire?" I asked.

"No. They are going to do an autopsy to see if she died in the fire or if she died beforehand," she said.

I felt sick to my stomach. Making my way to the hallway bathroom, I kneeled to release all the food that I had just eaten. The door swung open, and Kamari walked in and shut the door behind him. Grabbing my hair, he pulled it into a ponytail so that it wasn't in my face.

"I can't believe that she is dead," I said out loud.

"Yeah, babe. She's gone, baby. I'm sorry," he said.

Coming out of the bathroom, everyone rushed to me, but I was more worried about my sister because she would never get the closure that she needed as to why she hated her so much. I walked over to my sister and grabbed her. We held one another and just cried. No one said anything. They just stared at us until we were ready to speak. Blessing, on the other hand, had plans of her own. Crawling over to where Asha and I were, she pulled at us so that one of us would pick her up. Asha bent down to pick her up, and as she came back up, Blessing had her hands on her face, wiping her tears away. She looked at me and did the same thing.

"I hate to break up this moment, but we have to get moving in order to get to the location before it gets dark," Kairo said.

"He's right, bae. We still have packing to do, and I need to make a couple errands while you're doing that," Mari said.

"Okay, let's get moving so we can meet at the house at six," Robi said.

We all got up to help clean the kitchen, and then everyone left at the same time.

"Bae, I'm going to empty the trash so it doesn't stank while we are gone," Mari said as I headed up to the room.

As I started pulling things out of the closet, my thoughts fell back on my mother and the horrible way that she went out. I felt bad for thinking about how she treated Asha while she was living. Asha would go out of her way to check on her, only to be met with negativity and envy. Shaking off those thoughts, I had to figure out how I was going to complete my assignment. It was due online by Saturday, and Kairo said that we couldn't have any electronics.

"Do you think that there will be some kind of computer or something at the house?" I asked.

"More than likely he will, that's why he told y'all to leave them here," he replied.

"Okay, cool. I have a couple assignments that will be due before we get back," I said.

I finished packing our things. Kamari ran off to do his errands while I emailed all my teachers to let them know that I wouldn't be in class this week. While he was gone, I took the time to simply sit there and let out my cries for my mother. Although she wasn't the typical mother, she still was my mother, and without her, I wouldn't be here.

I didn't have a way to contact Joe because he had entered the rehab program, and I couldn't find the card that he gave me. Then again, it probably wasn't a good idea to tell him something like this over the phone anyway. I had a headache, so I decided to lie down on the couch until Kamari returned, and it was time for us to leave.

I slept a good lil' while, and Kamari returned empty-handed.

"What you been up to?" I asked.

"I bought a couple toys for Blessing so she would have something to do. I grabbed a couple more snacks for us. I know Robi said she got some, but I picked up some of the things you like," he said.

"Aww, look at you thinking of me and the baby," I said, kissing him.

'You got everything packed?" he asked.

"Yes, everything is packed, and we are ready to go," I said.

Grabbing our bags, we locked the house up and took the elevator to the garage, putting our suitcases in the back. I opened the back door to see all the stuff that he had bought for Blessing. I noticed that there were a couple toys in there for an older child, and I realized that he had bought some for Monica's daughter also. It was still early in the day, so we still had a couple hours to kill before it was time for us to meet up.

When we made it there, it looked like we were the only ones that were anxious about getting over here. Tez and Monica, with her daughter, were here, and Robi, of course, was in the kitchen frying chicken.

Asha and Kairo hadn't made it here yet. I wanted to check in on her since she delivered me the news and see how she was doing. I knew my sister. She would put on a strong face, but once it finally hit her, I wanted to be the shoulder for her to cry on.

ASHA

I wasn't expecting Justice to take the new of Kandi's death so well. Her bond with Kandi was stronger than mine, so I expected her to be completely broken up about it. I was currently finishing up packing my things so that we could head over to Robi's house. As I was sitting on the floor, Kairo came into the room and sat in the chair in the corner and watched me in silence.

"I want to thank you for everything that you have done for me, because you didn't have to do it. You have been my rock over these last few months, and I don't know how I would've gotten through them if you weren't here," I said.

"It's nothing, baby. Thank you for letting me be there for you. I know I came on strong when we first met, and that I was because I thought you were like the others, but you quickly changed my mind," he responded.

"That was a cute little baby, wasn't it?" I asked.

"Yeah, she was pretty cute. It's fucked up that she has been born into her situation," he said.

"Yeah, Ms. Mary said that she will be there for about three months before they allow her to go home," I said.

I couldn't figure out why I was so intrigued by Ms. Mary's granddaughter. I wanted kids, but I wasn't ready to have them just yet, which was why I brushed Kairo off when he talked about babies.

"Asha, we are leaving in about twenty minutes. Let me take the dogs out," Kairo said.

Putting the final things that I needed in a bag, I went downstairs to make myself a drink. My nerves were on edge because I was worrying and stressed at the same damn time. When Kairo came back in the house, he went and grabbed my bag and put it into the car while I sat in the living room watching a rerun of *Living Single*.

"You ready, baby?" he asked, walking through the door.

"Yeah," I said.

I grabbed my purse and headed out the door. Kairo set the alarm, and we headed over to Robi's house. When we got there, it was two large vans with tinted windows parked outside of her house.

"What's this about?" I asked.

"I got a couple vans so everyone can ride together. Biggs is going to drive one, and Mar will drive the other," he said.

"That's a smart idea. It won't be so many cars leaving or following each other," I said.

Walking into the house, I smelled chicken and immediately got sick to my stomach. Running to the nearest bathroom because I felt like I was going to be sick, I turned on the water and splashed my face a couple times.

I started to feel better. When I walked out the bathroom, Kairo was standing there waiting for me.

"You straight?" he asked.

"Yeah, I got sick real quick," I replied.

"Asha, you ain't pregnant, are you?" Robi asked.

"No, ma'am," I replied.

Walking into the dining room, Justice was sitting at the table stuffing her face and Blessing was right beside her in her highchair, gumming on a bone.

"Is it good, baby?" I asked Blessing, trying to take away her bone.

"Girl, you know better than to try to mess with her food. She does not play when it comes to the chicken," Justice said.

Tez and Mari were sitting in the living room stuffing their faces while watching the game, or better yet cursing at the game. Robi had finished cooking and was cleaning up the kitchen. She had about three different coolers with all kinds of food inside of it.

"Robi, who is supposed to eat all this fool in this cooler?" I asked.

"Girl, we will be locked up in that house for a full week. Trust me, that food in the cooler will be eaten up," she replied.

"Mari went to the store also and grabbed a couple things," Justice said.

"I think y'all should be straight. If not, then Biggs can run to the store or something," Kairo said.

The guys started to get the food and coolers and loaded up the trucks so that he could head to the location. As we drove to the location, it took us about two hours to get to this huge house that was overlooking a lake. We were the only house in the area, and there was a security guard at the entrance of the land. We had to be sitting on about seven to eight acres of land. The house was huge, like one of those houses you would see in the magazines—large windows, long steps leading up the house, and a three-car garage so we didn't even have to get out of the truck until we were in the garage.

When we did exit the truck and walked into the house, we entered into a chef-model kitchen. I knew Robi was going to fall in love when she saw it.

"Oh my God! Kairo, this is how I want you to do my kitchen in the house!" she yelled.

"Ight, come on. Let me give y'all the tour of the house," he said.

Walking through the house, I was amazed at the details. There was a total of eight bedrooms, six bathrooms, a pool, sauna, and an exercise room. There was a man cave in the basement of the house that had just about every kind of game that you could think of. He had a flat-screen mounted on every wall that he could in the cave.

"Ight, so under this chair is a panic room," he said.

"What the hell we need a panic room for?" Robi asked.

"This is another safety measure. If you move this chair, it will reveal a door. Turn the handle and take the stairs down. There is enough room for fifteen people comfortably. There is food, electricity, and running water down there, as well as a phone if you need to use the room," he explained.

As we went back up the stairs, I was starting to get nervous with all the information that he was giving us. I felt sick to my stomach yet again. Running to the bath-room, I began to throw up. It wasn't like I had eaten any food recently to make me sick.

"Kairo, you sure you ain't get Asha pregnant?" Rob asked.

"Nah, not that I know of. I mean, I have been trying, but she ain't having it," he said.

Kairo

You damn right I been trying to get Asha pregnant. I'd be a fool not to. It wasn't like I was trying to trap her or anything like that, but we would make some beautiful kids though. I knew she had a thing that she wanted to accomplish and that wasn't being my baby momma. I felt her when she said that she wanted to be a wife. I wish more women would think like her instead of being a baby momma to a dope boy.

I wanted to make sure that I got everything out of the way before I settled down and made an honest woman of Asha. I knew I wanted to be with her because she was independent, smart, and easy to be around. As we all sat around, my mind went to what was about to go down. I hoped this nigga would do exactly what I wanted and that was come out of hiding with his weak ass. We were going to engage in a four-day killing spree, taking out all his team, so he had no choice but to stand in the paint and deal with the repercussions of his actions.

"You straight, big bro?" Mari asked.

"Yeah, I just hope shit goes as planned."

"Asha, come here," Robi said.

Sitting down on the couch, we all gathered around to listen to what was about to be said. Hell, Robi didn't tell me anything, so I was curious to know what this was about.

"So I talked to your father's side, and they would like to meet with you when we get back," she said.

"Oh, really," Asha replied.

"Yes. It took a minute to get everyone to get their dates together, so we will have something at my house. That way, you are comfortable," Robi said.

"Asha, that is great," Justice said.

I looked at Justice. I saw the sadness behind her smile. I wondered where the guy James was. I knew he was in a rehab, but he never told her where he was going. Tomorrow, I was going to have McCray do some research to see if he could find him. Everyone was spread all around the house, doing a little of everything. Biggs and Tez were in the man cave shooting pool. Justice and Miya were sitting on the sofa talking. Robi was in the kitchen, of course, pulling out snack foods for us. Asha and Monica were sitting on the back porch having a drink. I was wondering how she was feeling after getting the news that her family wanted to meet with her.

I went to lie on the bed and watch some SportsCenter and relax. I was going to head back to the city about three or four so that I could get ready. It wasn't a lot of bosses out there that would get their hands dirty, but I learned from Taj and Midnight; if I wanted something done, do it myself. I didn't even realize that I was sleep until Asha climbed on the bed, tugging on my shorts.

"What's up, bae?" I asked.

"I'm horny and want some dick," she replied.

"Well, handle it then," I responded.

Removing my shorts, I laid flat on my back. Easing

down on my wood, she sucked in the air as she adjusted to my rod. Once she was comfortable, she began to wind her hips in a circular motion. She was wet as hell, like she had been thinking about doing this for a long time. I removed her shirt to reveal her sports bra.

"Take that shit off, Ash," I said, referring to the sports bra.

Taking it off without skipping a beat, she threw it on the floor. Flipping her over so that I was on top, I spread her legs so that I had full access to the pussy. As I entered her, you could hear the gushing sound as I went in and out of her. The way she sucked me in when I entered her made me weak each and every time.

"If I want it out of this relationship that we in , let me know now because I'm marrying you, girl," I said.

I knew it had to be the pussy talking because I had never voiced that to anyone other than myself. Just as I was about to let go, Asha got her second wind and wanted to be adventurous.

"Bae, let's go on the balcony," she said.

"Ight," I replied.

Walking out on the balcony, she bent over the railing, giving me access to enter her from behind.

"Damn," she said as I entered her.

Matching my thrusts and throwing it back, we came at the same time after a few minutes. It was a good thing that our room was on the other side of the house, because if they could've heard me and Asha, they wouldn't be fucking with us for a long time. Sitting on the chaise lounge to catch my breath, Asha went into the bathroom to shower. It had to be about one o'clock in the morning. Tez and I said that we were leaving about three to make it back in town.

I joined Asha in the shower. I watched as she lathered up her body with soap as the water ran over her body.

"See something that you like?" she asked.

Licking my lips at her, I was now ready for round two. Kneeling so that I was now eye level with her kitty, I lifted her leg over my shoulder as she leaned against the shower wall. I let the water fall down my back as I devoured her in my mouth. She tasted like pineapples with a hint of vanilla from the bodywash. As I continued to give her the tongue-lashing of her life, she released down my throat a creamy treat.

Completely drained, she cleaned herself up and dried off to get into bed.

"I'm leaving in about an hour, so if you don't see me before I leave, just know that I love you, girl."

"Stop talking like that. You will make it back to me," she replied as she snuggled up to me.

I walked the entire house to check on everyone before I left. I let Mari know that I was leaving. He was sleep but was able to fully understand what I was saying. Dapping me, we said our love yous, and I left out of the room. The only person that was up was Robi. She was in a corner of the house kneeling down, praying. This had probably been the fifth or sixth time that I had actually seen Robi pray.

"Lord, I ask you to watch over my baby as they go out in these streets. Lord, I ask you to watch over them so that they can make it back to their families with no injuries to them. Protect them, Lord. Show them that it is more to life than what they are currently doing. Show them another way to live their lives so that they can become the men that they are destined to be."

I leaned against the wall as she finished praying. I felt everything that she was saying, and she knew me and my heart better than anyone else.

"Kairo, y'all about to leave?" she asked as tears started to fall.

"Come on, Robi. I need you to be strong. If you crack, then it's going to cause everyone else to follow suit. I love you, and I will see you in a couple days," I said as I kissed her on the cheek.

Tez and I jumped into the van. I had to take a breath to get myself together. I was about to stir some shit up, and the outcome could either go well for us or bad for us. I just hoped things worked out in our favor.

"Nigga, you ready?" Tez asked.

"Ready as I'll ever be. Nigga, is you ready?" I asked.

"You bet I am," he responded.

We started on our journey back to the city. It was the goal to make it back before the sun came up. We were meeting at the warehouse so that we could get the game plan together. We had niggas watching their block for days, so we knew when they switched shifts, where the drops were made, and the money house. I wanted it all, and I wasn't afraid to let them know who was responsible for this.

We dropped the truck back to my house so that we could pull out my heavy-duty SUV; it bulletproof everything. The same material that they made Obama's cars out of, that's what my truck was made out of. Nothing was getting through the doors or windows. I had an arsenal of weapons in the back of the truck. Anything that you could think of, I had it and the legal way also.

By the time that we made it to the warehouse, just about everyone was there. Blaze had made it with the crew that was under her. Taj, Kiah, and Night had made it there. A few of their guys had arrived the night before, so we were about thirty strong. We weren't planning on moving until about five or six, so we had plenty of time.

"Look, I want to thank each and every one of you that is about to go to war with this little nigga. If y'all know anything about me, it is my family and loyalty is the most important thing to me," I said.

"Nigga, cut all that mushy shit out. Let's get to work!" Taj shouted.

"Nigga, fuck you!" I shouted back.

We worked out the details, and while my and Night's men worked out the final details, I went upstairs to my office to gather my thoughts.

"You straight up here, bro?" Taj asked.

"Yeah, I just want to know what the lil' nigga want? I want to know was it worth you losing your life?" I asked.

"Niggas are envious of the bosses and will do anything in their power to try to remove you from the top," Taj said.

"You would've thought niggas would've learned from playing with me a couple years ago."

"Well, I guess it is time to remind them who the fuck you are," he said.

"Alright, so we all set. It's on for eight o'clock. We are hitting the stash house and money house first. While they're hitting the houses, we will be taking out the corner boys. Blaze has the location of the second in charge. You, Taj, and Night, grab his ass."

"Well, it looks like you have everything worked out here. Let's go grab me something to eat," I replied.

We all piled into the cars and trucks that we brought, and we headed to the diner that I had taken Asha to. I had called on the way to let the owner know that we were arriving with about thirty people. I had given them some money so that they could expand the diner, no strings attached. The owner told me that he would have a spot for me and my friends at any time.

By the time that we made it there, the expansion was completely empty, and we all sat down as everyone else waited in line. Because it was such a large party, we had about four or five waitresses serving us. Of course, one of the servers would have to be one of the bitches that I had fucked and never called again to serve us.

"Well, if it isn't Mr. No-Call Budah," she said.

"What's up, Shanice?"

"You lost my number or something?" she asked.

"Nah, I didn't lose it. I just choose not to use it again."

"So you can hit and then don't call again," she said,

"Damn, you must've put that Stevie J on her ass," Taj laughed.

"Look, now isn't the time or place to have this discussion, but if you want to have it, let's go. You weren't that fucking special. You see the money and the cars and instantly see dollar signs. You wanted to give me the pussy in a nightclub. You think that's the kind of woman I want on my arm? Nah. My wife is always a lady in the street. Now, if you don't mind, I would like to have someone else take my order," I stated.

"Well, damn. You just crushed her little soul," Night said, laughing.

"Nah, I'm trying to do right. I'll be damned if I mess shit up with Asha off some slide I smashed before she was thought about," I said.

"Nigga, is that growth I see on you? It looks good," Taj said.

"Nigga, whatever!" I laughed.

We all sat in the diner for a good two hours, eating and talking shit. Night and I paid the tab for everyone, and I went back to my house to take a nap. I wanted badly to talk to Asha to see how she and everyone were doing since I left while everyone was sleeping. I decided that I was going to give Mari a call. I had given him a burner phone to use in case of emergency.

"What's up, Mari?" I asked.

"Shit, what's up? Robi in here working everyone's nerves trying to feed everyone." He laughed.

"Where Asha at, man? I want to holla at her real quick."

"She's in the pool. Hold on. Yo, Ash! Come get the phone!" he yelled.

"Hello," she sang in her sweet voice.

"What's up, baby?"

"Why you didn't wake me when you left?" she asked.

"- If I would've woke you up before I left you would've started all that crying. It was better that way,"

"What you are doing?" she asked.

"Just got home from eating, about to take a nap. I just called to hear your voice," I said.

"I miss you," she said

"I miss you too. See you soon."

With that, I hung up the phone. I had to lie down to get my mind right but not before I set my alarm for four thirty. I woke up to my phone ringing, letting me know that it was time for me to get up. The house seemed so empty with Asha not being here. As I was walking to the shower, I received a text from McCray, letting me know that he had the information that I wanted. I sent him a text back that I would get with him in the morning.

I texted everyone that I would be at the warehouse in thirty minutes and it would be go time. I shitted, shaved, and showered, threw on my all black with some Timbs, and was out the door. I was ready to get this shit over and have my family back home living their lives.

By the time that I made it to the warehouse, everyone was there loading up their cars and trucks. Night, Taj, and I took my truck and waited on the others. We were following Blaze because she knew where the second in charge was. As we were driving to the location, the area looked familiar. It wasn't until we pulled up to the house that I realized where we were. We were parked outside of Ameka's house. I had dropped her ass off there a time or two.

This bitch was doing all of that and was fucking the enemy the whole time. I wanted to kick her door in and fuck her and him up, but I had to remain calm and focused. Blaze texted me and said that he should be coming out of the house in ten minutes, and just like clockwork, the door opened, and he walked out the door with Ameka behind him.

"I can't believe this shit here," I said out loud.

"Nigga, what you are talking about?' Taj asked.

"That's the bitch that jumped Asha with her moms."

I called Blaze and told her to stay back and grab Ameka. I told her to make sure that no one saw her when she did it. Meanwhile, we followed the nigga to see where he was going. This nigga went to grab something to eat and then went to another house that had some kids playing outside. When he pulled up, the kids ran to the car to hug him and a woman stood at the door waiting for him. He walked up to the door, kissing the woman that was standing there.

"This nigga a pimp," Taj said.

We waited at the house for about twenty minutes before he came out of the house and jumped back into the car. We followed him into a parking lot. I let Taj out of the truck so that he could sneak up on him, and just as he was about to walk away from the car, Taj came up from behind with a gun to the back of his head. We pulled up and forced him into the truck. We didn't give a fuck if he saw our faces or not. He wouldn't live to see another day anyway.

We drove his ass back to the warehouse. The entire time that we were driving, he was rapping.

"Do you know who the fuck I am?" he asked.

"Frankly, I don't give a fuck," I replied.

"You're a dead man! You know that?" he responded.

"Is that supposed to scare me? Do it look like I give a fuck, because I don't?"

As we were pulling into the warehouse, he continued with his rant, which none of us were paying attention to anyway.

"Do you know who the fuck I am?" he asked.

"No, motherfucker, do you know who I am?" I responded.

"Nigga, once we are done with you, you will wish that you would've listened," he spat.

"Nigga, I fear no man, Aaron, second-in-command of this little petty ass crew that is run by that fuck nigga, Nasir. You fuckers chose to fuck with my brother and for what? I don't even know who the fuck y'all are. But I'll bet this on my unborn child. By the time I'm done, if you don't know about me, you will when I'm finished," I stated.

With that, Taj put two to his dome, and he was dead. I didn't have time to fuck around with these no-name ass niggas. I needed them out of the way and out of my way fast. Blaze sent me a text that she was on her way with Ameka and would here in five minutes. Oh, this should be fun to see the look on her face when she saw this nigga lying on the floor in his own blood.

MARI

Robi was working all my nerves trying to feed everyone because she was stressed. I tried to get her to lie down a couple times, but each time that she did, she would be in her room for about a good twenty minutes, and then she would be back out of her room, fucking with people again. I was chilling on the back porch while everyone was in the pool. Robi was still stressing and worrying me to death. I tell you what though—if she said one more thing about food, I was pushing her ass in the pool—clothes and all. Hell, she would just have to be mad at me.

When Kairo called, Asha's face lit up just from the sound of his voice. I could tell that she really loved my brother. Justice was sitting on the side of the pool, acting like she didn't want to get in. The whole vibe at the house was off, so I decided to turn on some music to lighten the mood and have some fun.

"Robi, you going to throw something on the grill since you keep trying to feed us?" I asked.

"I can if you ask nicely," she replied.

I walked past her and straight over to Justice and pushed her into the pool. She was mad as hell at me, but what was the point of sitting there if you weren't going to get in?

"Mari, I'm going to kick your ass!" Justice yelled.

Asha and Monica were laughing their ass off while sitting on the chair. I wasn't sure what Asha's ass was laughing about because she was next, and she didn't even know it. I walked up behind her and picked her up and threw her into the pool. Monica tried to get up and run, but I was hot on her trail. I scooped her up, and we both ended up in the pool this time because Robi pushed me. I was trying my best to get everyone's mind off what the others were engaging in, and it looked like I had succeeded.

The rest of the day, we chilled around the house with the music playing. Robi was on the grill and getting in and out of the pool. I had estimated that Kairo and Tez would be back here in two days. That way, it would give them time to see if there was going to be any buzz about who was responsible for the killings. We had cable at the house, so I was able to watch what was going on from afar, but I decided not to watch it around the ladies because they would start with the million and one questions.

Looking down at my phone, I received a text from Kendra asking what size did Blessing wear and that she wanted to buy her a couple things. I chose not to respond because that would've opened the door for her to ask about seeing her or start with the questions that I didn't have time for.

Biggs was walking the grounds to make sure that everything was secure. He was good with things like that. I had to pour me a drink to ease my mind because I was worried about my brother and family, although I didn't show it. I had to be strong for the ladies in the house. They were watching my every move.

I walked into Kairo's office, where there were surveillance cameras of all the property. Closing and locking the door, I turned on the news to get an update. There wasn't any news of the bloodshed reporting, but there was a story of a body being found with no arms and legs; it was just the torso with no head.

When I heard that, I knew that this was Kairo's doing. Only he would do something like that so that Tyshawn's family would be able to say their goodbyes to the snitch. He was crazy when it came to making others suffer or inflicting pain on others. It was like he enjoyed it or something. Coming out of the office, I ran into Biggs. He gave me the overview of the property, telling me that there were no changes since we arrived and that he would check again before we turned in for bed.

When I walked into the living room, everyone was having a conversation about something. When they saw me, they quickly changed the subject like they didn't want me to know what they were talking about.

"What the hell y'all staring at me like that for?" I asked.

Miya busted out laughing, and everyone followed behind her giggling. Shaking my head, I walked over to the bar to pour me another drink. Dealing with all these women was enough to drive me insane. The only person that was acting like she had some sense was Blessing, and she was just sitting there watching them.

"So Mari, what all do you have planned for Justice?" Monica asked.

"Touch your nose, lil' nosy," I replied.

"Come on. Give us some details of this main event. This is my sister's big day, so she has to slay," Asha said.

"She will be straight. Don't worry about that. I got her," I responded.

I walked into the kitchen, grabbed me something to eat, and headed down to the man cave because I needed to relax with all these damn women. Biggs was down there eating and watching SportsCenter.

"Nigga, hook up the game. I want to see what that Fortnite about," I said to him.

We hooked up the game and spent hours down there. I could hear the ladies upstairs, singing songs and cheering each other on. I was assuming that they were dancing around the house. After a couple hours, the house became silent. We paused the game to go check and see what was going on. To our surprise, everyone was laid out on the couches and floor. Blessing was in her chair sleeping also.

I picked up Blessing and carried her to her crib and came back and woke up the rest of everyone. Robi, the hardhead, acted like she wasn't sleeping but went ahead to bed also. Once I finished getting everyone settled, I went back to the man cave to finish the game.

We played the game for another couple hours, and then, we went to bed. Crawling into bed, Justice was all over the bed. Her hair was all over the place because she hadn't tied it up. Taking a shower, I got in the bed and pulled her close to me and fell asleep instantly.

When I woke up the next morning, I woke up to Blessing slobbering on my face and Justice still sleeping.

"Justice, you put her in the bed?" I asked.

"Yeah. I put her in the bed about ten minutes ago," she replied.

Getting up out of bed to relieve myself, Justice came in and turned on the shower and got in. I was shocked that she had done that because she hadn't done that before. Walking out to see what was going on in the rest of the house, Asha was sitting on the back porch zoning.

"Morning, Asha."

"Morning, bro," she replied.

"You straight this morning?" I asked.

"Yeah. I was feeling good last night."

"Yeah, I see you were. Matter fact, you all were." I laughed.

As I was about to walk back into the house, Robi came outside telling us that she was about to cook breakfast. I was glad she came out because I was about to go fix me a bowl of cereal. Biggs walked into the house out of breath like he had been running, and that made me nervous.

"What's the matter with you?" I asked.

"Nothing, I went for a morning run," he replied.

Robi was in the kitchen whipping up food while I went into the office, locked the room, and turned on the news. They were reporting on the recent murders of six people in the area of Nasir's territory. They were stating that they didn't have any leads, and the police were looking for witnesses and information. I turned on the other news channel and they were talking about another shooting of four people in a car that were found sitting on the block.

I could tell that it had been a busy night for Kairo and the crew. I think that they said that the crew total was about twenty to twenty-five, and I knew Kairo's goal was to kill them all. I sat in the office for about an hour and watched the camera. I watched as different cars passed by the main road and watched what the security guards was doing, or in other words, weren't doing. Robi knocked on the door to let me know that the food was ready and to come and eat. When I walked into the kitchen, you would've thought that we were in an all-you-can-eat restaurant. Robi cooked everything that you could think of and had it sitting on the counter.

As we sat down to eat, I received another call from Kairo. He was talking in codes, but he was basically telling me that everything was going as planned and it should be over in a day or so. The conversation was short and straight to the point, just the way it had always been when shit was hot.

JUSTICE

I would be glad when we got back to our normal lives. Between Mari and Kairo talking in codes on the phone and us being held in this big ass house, it was enough to drive me crazy. I went to the living room with my books and put them on the table. I had to study for my final that I had coming up, and it was a must that I aced this exam. I still hadn't received my acceptance letters from the other schools that I was waiting on. I was really waiting to hear from John Hopkins which was my first choice, but if I didn't hear from them, UPenn was my second choice anyway which as still a great school.

As I was sitting there, Miya joined me at the table with her books, and we had a small study session while the others went on to do other things. I was still in my feelings about the passing of Kandi. I walked to talk to Asha to see if we were going to do something small for her. I knew that they didn't have the best relationship, but she still was her mother.

"Justice, are you a virgin?" Miya asked.

Not saying a word, I acted like I hadn't heard her.

"Heifer, don't act like you don't hear me/ Answer the question," she said.

I was assuming that she read my body language and silence and got her answer that she was looking for.

"Come with me," she said, taking my hand.

We went into her room and sat on the couch at the end of her bed.

"Justice, I know that you are a virgin, and I know that you are probably going to give yourself to my brother, but I want you to do it because you want to and not because he is forcing you to, because I will kick his ass. Big brother or not, I know that life hasn't been easy, but don't do anything unless you are ready," she said.

"Miya, are you a virgin?" I asked.

"Up until about two weeks ago, and believe me, it isn't all that they make it seem to be," she responded.

"You and Javon?" I asked shockingly.

"Yeah, girl, and you better not tell my brother because they will kill both him and I," she replied.

We walked back into the dining room to finish studying when Asha and Monica walked in to see what we were up to. They both had on their bathing suits, and Justice and Paris had on theirs also.

"What y'all in here doing? We about to get in the pool," Monica said.

"We will come once we finish. We have about twenty minutes left to do," Miya said.

They walked back out the dining room and went out back. Mari walked past me with his basketball shorts on with no shirt, revealing his deep V at his midsection. Just the sight of him caused my juices to flow ,and I had to squeeze my legs tight. As he stood behind Miya staring at me, it made me even hornier than I was already.

"Justice, y'all getting in the pool?" he asked.

Licking my lips, I nodded my head because I couldn't speak at the moment. He stood there for a couple more moments watching me, and then he walked out back. Miya and I finished studying, and I headed to put my books up, when Mari appeared out of nowhere. Closing the door behind him, he locked the door.

"Justice, I got to have you ma," he said as he walked up to me.

Kissing me intensely, his hands roamed my body as I pulled the strings to reveal his already-erect manhood.

"Nah, baby, not like that," he said.

Lying me back on the bed, he removed my shorts, revealing my kitty. Kneeling so that he was eye level with my kitty, he spread my legs. He began to slowly suck on my clit. The sensation alone caused me to cover my face so no one could hear my moans. Mari was a beast when it came to my needs. He always handled me with care and never forced me to go any further than I wanted to.

I was grabbing the pillows, sheets, everything that I could get my hands on to keep from letting out the loud moans. Mari stood up, picked up his phone, and connected it to the Bluetooth speaker so that the music was playing loud to cover my moans. As he went back to murdering my kitten, I was able to finally voice my pleasure without feeling some kind of way. After about ten more minutes, I couldn't hold it in any longer. The next thing I knew, I did something that scared the hell out of me. It felt like I was peeing on myself, and Mari was just as shocked as me.

"Baby, I'm sorry. I just peed on you!" I shouted.

"Shhhh, you straight, and it's not pee. Some women have a talent that when they cum, it comes out looking and feeling like pee," he replied.

Getting up off the bed, I walked into the bathroom room to clean myself up. I was completely ashamed of what had just happened, and although Mari tried to ensure that he was fine, I still felt like shit.

When I walked out of the bathroom, Mari was lying on the bed watching TV like nothing had just happened.

"Get up so I can throw these covers in the washer," I said.

"Girl, you are tripping, the bed ain't even wet. Most of it got on the food," he replied.

Finally getting up, I grabbed the covers of the bed and went to the laundry room. When I returned, I put my bathing suit on and went outside with the others. When I walked out back, Myia looked at me crazy while Asha and Monica were giving me the side eye, like I had a sign on my forehead saying that I squirted for the first time.

Robi came out with her glass in her hand with her bathing suit on. I had to laugh because you couldn't tell her anything with her little two-piece that she had on.

"Robi, where your damn clothes at?" Mari asked.

"Boy, mind your damn business. I'm grown around this bitch," she replied.

We all started laughing because Mari had his nose turned up like he was disgusted, but Robi actually looked good for her age.

We stayed out by the pool until the sun began to set, and then we went into the house to play some games while Asha cooked dinner. It was like she and Robi were taking turns stressing, and when Asha stressed, it was completely different. She automatically became an iron chef and wanted to experiment with different things and spices.

She ended up cooking herb-seasoned salmon with jasmine rice, which happened to be my favorite.

"Asha, baby, this is good, girl. You have to give me your recipe for this," Robi said.

"Yeah, I'll give you the recipe for it," she replied.

We all sat at the table and ate like it was the last supper. When we were finished, I went and cleaned up the kitchen while Mari bathed Blessing and put her down for bed. By the time that I made it in the room, he and Blessing both were knocked out. I climbed into bed and fell asleep with them in no time.

ASHA

Today was a good day, but I was missing Kairo like crazy. I never knew that I would miss him so much until this happened. I was lying in the bed watching a movie and thinking about all the thinking I had to do once I got back. I had to go and identify Kandi's body and begin the funeral arrangements. She didn't have a lot of family and friends, so it would probably just a same-day service.

I was not sure when I drifted off to sleep, but I dreamed that Kairo had made it back and that he was whispering in my ear that he loved me. When I turned over and felt the side of the bed, I realized that it was, in fact, a dream and went back to sleep mad. The sun came up earlier than I wanted it to. I had spent most of my night tossing and turning in bed. I was up and down because of all the liquor I had drank throughout the day.

The smell of breakfast caused me to get out of bed. Walking into the bathroom, I relieved myself, washed my face, and brushed my teeth. As I was about to jump in the shower, I could've sworn that I had heard Kairo's laugh, but it was my mind playing tricks on me. I had my Pandora playing as I got in the shower. The music was bumping this morning as I lathered my body. The next thing I knew, the shower door opened, and in walked Kairo.

Standing there completely shocked, we immediately embraced each other and engaged in a deep, passionate kiss. Picking me up with ease, he placed his erect manhood inside on me with one quick motion. Locking my legs around his hip, I bucked on him like this was the last piece of dick that I was going to get in a long time.

"Shit, Ash, you missed me, huh?" he said.

"Hell yes! Damn, this dick is just what I needed," I replied.

Letting out the loudest longest moan that I had ever experienced, I released my buildup, and Kairo came at the same time that I did. Getting out of the shower, we laid on the bed wet, and we laid there as the music played.

"I don't believe, we were put together not to be together,

And I don't believe, there's anyone out there that can love me better,

I don't believe, that you know how much I miss seeing your pretty smile.

Of course we had our ups and downs, but I gotta have you around me, cuz...

I feel it all over my body. I dream about you when I sleep .

You're the one for me. You're the one for me.

All the signs say, that ever since the day that we laid eyes on each other, baby,

You're the one for me. You're the one for me"

"Baby, this is the song I want to be played when we get married," Kairo said.

"Well, when is this supposed to happen? I asked.

"Soon. I was thinking about once you finish nursing school," he replied.

"I know this isn't what you call proposing?" I asked.

"Naw. We are just talking about our wedding," he replied.

"Oh, OK. Well, I want a destination wedding to Hawaii," I stated.

"Anything for you. No limits to what you can have."

"Who was cooking downstairs?" I asked.

"That was me and Tez, but no one came downstairs, so we called ourselves waking up the house, but you see how that went."

I jumped up and threw on the shorts and a tank top and told him to come on. The first place I went was to check on the baby, but she wasn't in her room. I knocked on Mari and Justice's bedroom and told them to give me Blessing, and we went back to my room. Kairo was still lying on the bed, but he now had on clothes though.

"Look who is here, B."

"There goes my baby. Come here, little munchkin."

As soon as Blessing saw her uncle, her eyes lit up. I admired the relationship that they had. I didn't have any aunts or uncles growing up that I could hang out with or look up to, so it was a joy to watch the two of them. Kairo was able to be as silly as he wanted when it came to Blessing, and she would just laugh at him. I wondered would he be like that if he was to have kids. Would he be the good father that wanted the best for his kids and go over and above for them?

Getting up off the bed, him and Blessing walked down to the kitchen to eat. I was in the middle of fixing his plate when Robi walked into the kitchen.

"Damn, you beat me to it," she said.

"Nah, I bet you to it," Kairo said.

"Shit, boy, you scared me," she said, walking over to him and kissing his cheek.

With that, it seemed like everyone was coming down one by one and was surprised that Kairo and Tez had made it back so soon. We all ate at the table, and we decided that, once Justice graduated, we were going on a vacation. I wanted to go the Bahamas, so everyone agreed that we would do that. I wasn't feeling good after I ate, so I went and laid down. My stomach was messed up. I was assuming from all the drinking I had been doing in the last few days.

There was a knock at the door, and then Justice walked through the door.

"Ash, you okay?" she asked.

"Yeah, my stomach is bothering me. What's up?"

"So what are we going to do about burying Kandi?" she asked.

"I was going to ask you what you wanted to do, and we would make the arrangements together, if you were up to it."

"I wanted to get in touch with James because I don't think that we should tell him over the phone," she said.

"Yeah, I think it would be best if we told him face-to-face and let the facility know also so they can help him deal with it."

"I wonder if Kairo or Mari can have someone find him for us," she said.

"I can see if Kairo can. I'm sure he has a way of finding people."

"Okay, when we get back, we can go ahead and plan the service and stuff. Of course, it will be a closed casket because she was burnt," Justice said.

Kairo came into the room to check on me while Justice was still there, so we asked him to find James, which he told us that he had someone looking for him, and as soon as he was found, we would know. As he was talking, his phone rang, and he went to the balcony to take the call.

KAIRO

"What's up?" I asked.

"I found the person you were looking for," McCray said.

"Ight, where is he?"

"He is about six hours away from here. I'll send you the address when we get off the phone. Oh, I got a lead also on Asha's mom's death. Word on the street is that Ameka and the nigga Nasir had something to do with it," he stated.

"What you mean Ameka and Nasir?" I asked.

"Well, apparently, she and him have something going on, as well as his second in command."

"Wait, so she fucking the both of them? They know about this shit too?" I asked.

"I'm guessing, but I can't confirm that they know about each other."

"That bitch was slimy as fuck. Good looking out!" I responded.

"I'll send you the address in a few."

I'll hit you up when I get back in town," I stated.

Hanging up from McCray, I went back in to tell Asha and Justice that I had an address from James and that we could go see him when they got ready. It was about three hours from where we were. I was going to call ahead and let the facility know that we had to see him and that it was a family emergency.

Justice walked out of the room to go get dressed while Asha sat there for a moment. I could tell that she was upset that she wasn't able to fix the issues that she and her mother had before she died.

"Asha, don't beat yourself up about the issues y'all had. The issues that she had were within herself, those were her demons that didn't allow her to heal or even love when it came to you," I said.

"I know, and it's fucked up because I tried on more than one occasion, and the repayment I got was being cursed out and her stooping so low as to be a part of people jumping me," she said with tears.

"Look, all you can do now is bury her and let all the pain go. I know it sounds harsh, but that is the only way that you will be able to prosper."

"I know you're right. It is easier said than done though," she said.

"It's going to take time, but we will get through this together."

As she walked into the bathroom to do something to her hair, I texted my jeweler and let them know that I needed to come see them because I wanted to have Asha's ring custom made. She was unique and special in my eyes, so it was only right that I got her a ring that was equally unique and special.

I went downstairs and told Robi what the play was, and Mari agreed with me that he should come along and that Robi was going to stay and watch Blessing. After about thirty minutes, Asha and Justice came downstairs ready to go. We all jumped in my truck that I had brought back and headed out. I tried to lighten the mood, because it was really heavy, by talking to Justice about going off to school, but her answers were short. Asha looked like she was staring off in space thinking. So Mari and I just talked while they sat in the back silent.

The ride felt like it was shorter than the three hours that he drove. I had Asha and Justice sit in the truck while Mari and I went and talked to the administrators of the facility. They agreed to let us speak with James and informed us that they would have a staff member there also to help him deal with the news that we were about to give him.

We walked out to the truck and told Asha and Justice to come in. We were taken to a conference room. James was currently in one of his meetings, and we had about a twenty-minute wait, so we all sat there looking crazy. Mari reached into his pockets and gave Asha and Justice their phones back. As soon as they powered their phones on, they received notifications for about five minutes each.

Justice busted out laughing at one of the messages that she had received.

"Drea threatened to call the police and report me missing if she didn't hear from me, but that was three days ago," she said.

"Guess you should go ahead and let her know that you are alright." Asha giggled.

"I'll call her after we leave here," she replied.

We sat there for a couple minutes more. When the door opened, James appeared.

"If you two are here, that must mean you have to tell me some damn news," James said, sitting down.

We sat there for a couple minutes silent while Asha and Justice stared at him. Taking a deep breath, Asha began to speak.

"Well, James, you are correct. We have some bad news to give you, and we felt like we had to tell you in person," Asha said.

"I know it has to do with Kandi. What did she do?" he asked.

"James, Kandi is dead. She was found in a house on the north side that caught on fire," Justice said.

"What do you mean dead?" he asked.

"Yes. I received a call a couple days ago letting me know that she was dead. They were trying to rule out foul play, but it looks like she died before the fire, and someone tried to cover it up," Asha said.

"I told her time and time again about running off with people that she didn't know, but she wouldn't listen," he sobbed.

This shit was heartbreaking because you could see the pain on his face. Asha had told me that James had wanted Kandi to come along to the center to get clean also, but he couldn't find her. Asha and Justice got up and came around the table and hugged James while the staff worker watched on.

"James, I want you to know that when you get clean and make it home, I have a job waiting for you so that you can keep on the road to sobriety," I stated.

"I appreciate that, man. I really do. I know that it will be hard for me to find work because of my addiction, but I'm ready to hit the ground running,' he replied.

"Will you be able to make it to the service? We can come and get you and bring you back if we need to. You two spent a lot of years together, so it's only right that you are there as we lay her to rest," Asha said.

"I will speak with the administration and see what they say. I might have to bring someone along with me to help keep me straight."

"You tell us what you need, and we will get it together," James said to the staff worker.

"We will have the information that you need in the next day or so. When is the service?" the gentleman asked.

"I have to get back home to make the arrangements, but I am hoping for next week Friday or Saturday," Asha said.

"Okay. Once you get all the information together, give me a call so that we can coordinate together. More than likely, I will be the one that will be escorting him down," he said.

"I'm sorry, I didn't get your name," Asha said.

"I'm sorry. I'm Bradley Williams, one of the therapists here at the facility," he stated.

I sat and watched James, and I could tell that he was hurting. I asked could I speak with him alone, and the therapist agreed.

We walked outside the office and down the hall toward the garden that was outside. Mari had come along also, leaving Asha and Justice to talk to Mr. Williams.

"I can see that you are taking this kind of hard. What's up?" I asked.

"I just feel bad that I left her out there and didn't go and look for her because I was so pissed at her," he stated.

"My dude, you aren't responsible for what happened to her. The motherfucker that did this to her is, and trust me, we will find out who was responsible," Mari said.

"I really appreciate y'all looking out for Asha and Justice. They didn't have the best upbringing when it came to Kandi. Asha didn't suffer too long, but Justice did," James said.

"We got them, trust that. They don't want for nothing, and we are there for you also. Just get yourself together because Justice is still going to need you. You're her pops," I stated.

We walked back into the office, where the girls were still talking to Mr. Williams.

"I think that we are finished here. We are going to head out, so once we get back home, we will call with the details," Asha said.

We said our goodbyes while Justice and Asha hugged James goodbye, and we headed out to the truck. When we got in the truck, Justice and Asha both said that James looked healthy and was completely different from the person that they had known before he entered the rehab. The drive back was so much lighter than the ride up—everyone was talking and joking around.

MARI

I was glad that I was able to be there for Justice when she went to see her father. She had been going through it, but once she saw him, it was like her mood had lightened up. When we made it back to the house, there was music playing, and Robi was in the house with Midnight, Kiah, and Taj. I had given them the address to come up and hang out before they headed out in a couple. It would give them a time to relax and get a feel for Asha and Justice and give Mari and I their input. I trusted their input, so whatever vibe they got off of them I would go from there.

"Aye, my nigga, how you invite us up, and then you ain't even here?" Taj said.

"Naw, I had to handle something with Asha and her sister," I replied.

"Don't worry. We kept my babies entertained and fed. Ain't that right, Monica?" he said.

I looked over at Taj, and he was staring down Monica.

I had seen that look before when he was single; he was trying to fuck Monica behind Tez's back.

"Aye, my nigga, cut it," I said.

Taj knew exactly what I was talking about because his whole mood changed, and he went on about his business. Justice and Asha went upstairs to change their clothes and came back downstairs. The first thing that they did was go into the kitchen to see if Robi and Monica needed any help. She told them no, so they joined us on the patio sitting at the other table by the pool.

"So tell me about yourself," Midnight said to Justice.

"I'm a senior in school like Miya. I'm hoping to attend John Hopkins in the fall, but if I don't, I have a backup school of UPenn," she replied.

"UPenn is a really good school. Plus, it's in my city, so you definitely will be okay," Midnight said.

"Oh, you live in Philadelphia?" she asked.

"Yeah, with my wife and three kids. We have been married for four years," he replied.

What Justice and Asha didn't know was when we went on our vacation, Taj and Midnight's family would be joining us also. I knew I had been waiting for the right person to bring around Yah and Keta because they both were a handful, but Asha and Justice could handle those two.

"So when do y'all leave out?" Asha asked.

"We are leaving out tomorrow night to get back home. I have a couple closings that I have to take care of when I get back," Midnight said.

"Oh, okay," she replied.

"I want to extend condolences on the loss of your mother. I know firsthand about rocky relationships between mother and daughters. My wife and her mother had one," he replied.

"Oh, really? Maybe she will give me some tips on how to deal with her loss," Asha said.

"Most definitely," he replied.

We all sat out on the back and just relaxed; we didn't have to stress or worry about Kairo not returning home. We just chilled and took in the vibe and atmosphere. The fellas and I stayed up late, just talking about life and what we saw in our future. Kairo sprung something on me that I didn't expect though. He said that in a couple years, he would fall back and let Tez, Blaze, and I be on the front while he chilled in the back.

When he said that, I didn't know what to think. He said that the goal was to not give your entire life to the game. We needed to start branching out and forming businesses to seem legit, and for the most part, I had my name in the work field.

I turned into bed after we finished the conversation. Justice was all over the bed with Blessing right up under her. I knew that it was a lot for her to deal with me, let alone take care of my daughter with me. I knew most chicks her age would've walked away from me by now. Dealing with a crazy ass baby momma, her mother, and then the lifestyle that I was living was completely different than what she used to, but she was adjusting well.

ASHA

I was glad that we were able to get ahold of James and let him know what had happened to Kandi. I knew that he felt bad because my grandmother always thought he was the reason that my mother got turned on to drugs, but from what the therapist was telling me, it was the other way around.

He told us that when my mother met him, he was a real estate agent on the north side that had just gotten out of a relationship. When I found out the information, I felt bad because my grandmother would never know the real story of what went down. I was in the bed listening to music while Kairo and the men were out on the patio, being loud of course. I was trying to wait up for him, but he was taking too long, and my head and stomach were hurting, so I went ahead to sleep.

I felt Kairo when he came into bed. He kissed me on my cheek and pulled me close to him and inhaled my hair. I was sleeping great until there was a knock at the bedroom door. It was Monica at the door, asking me if I had any Aleve because she had a headache. I quietly got out of the bed so that I wouldn't wake up Kairo, and she and I headed downstairs.

"Girl, you and Kairo seem pretty serious," she said.

"It didn't dawn on me how much I care for him until he was gone and his life was in danger," I replied.

"That man is in love with you. It's written all over his face."

"You think so? I mean, I know that he is feeling me and all, but to be in love? I just think that he is in like with me," I replied.

"Girl, keep thinking like that. I know Tez feeling me, but y'all two are on a different level," Monica said.

"I don't know, girl. I just want to start school and get it over with. I think I want to work with the babies," I said.

"I could see that with you. It takes a special person to be able to work with babies and children," she replied.

"What y'all out here doing?" Justice said with a cup in her hand.

"We just talking about school and whether or not I'm going to specialized in that department," I said.

"I think that would be dope. I want to be an OB doctor. OMG! It would be so cool if I had a practice with Miya and you and Monica be our nurses," Justice said excitedly.

"Yeah, that would be kind of fly to have an all-family practice," Monica said.

"So what's the plan for today because I have got to get out of the fucking house?" Miya said, walking out.

"Excuse me, ma'am," I replied.

"I'm sorry, Ash, but damn," she said, laughing.

"You betta not let ya brothers hear you cursing. You know they think you are an angel," Justice said.

"I'm saying though. Are we hitting the mall or something?" Justice said.

"Let me talk to Kairo and let him know that we are going shopping," I said.

"Yeah, you do that. You know what he likes; we don't." Monica laughed.

As we were sitting on the porch, it looked like everyone started to come alive and come out one by one. Eventually, the whole house was on the back porch, trying to get themselves together from the night before. Robi was drinking her coffee, Taj had a Corona in his hand, and Kairo was staring at me like it was just him and I in the house.

"Damn, nigga, she yours!" Kiah said.

"Whatever," he responded.

"Bae, we were thinking about going to the mall. We have been stuck in the house forever," I said, sitting on Kairo's lap.

"Oh, word? Just pick me something up fly," he said.

I went back into the house so that I could throw my clothes in the washer and take a shower so we could head out once we were finished getting dressed. We were so anxious to get to the mall that we didn't even eat breakfast.

As I was getting dressed, Kairo walked into the room and laid across the bed.

"What's the matter?" I asked.

"Nothing. I'm just chilling. When are you going to meet your other side?" he asked.

"Once I get everything situated with Kandi, I'll arrange to meet with them," I said.

"You ready, sis," Justice said, standing at the door.

"Just about. Give me five more minutes," I replied.

As I was grabbing my purse and taking my phone off the charger, Kairo reached into his wallet and handed me a credit card.

"Bae, I don't need your credit card. I have money," I said.

"That isn't my credit card; it's your credit card," he replied.

Looking down at the card, it did, in fact, have my name on it. It was an American Express Black, so I knew there was no limit on it. Sticking the card in my purse, I jumped on the bed to give him a kiss goodbye. When I walked downstairs, everyone was ready: Robi, Miya, Justice, Blessing, Monica, and Paris.

"There they go about to break a nigga's pocket. The mall better beware," Mari said.

"Yep, so you better get ready for this bill, right, Justice?" Robi said.

I noticed that Justice was quiet with her response. I was wondering what was wrong with her. Once we made it out of the door, I pulled Justice to the side to see what was wrong with her.

"Justice, what is the matter?" I asked.

"I'm not sure, sis. Mari has been nothing but a gentleman to me, and I'm just wondering how long this fairy tale will last," she replied.

"Girl, if you don't stop overthinking everything with Mari, I'm going to hurt you. Mari is feeling you without a doubt. I have learned from this man that they only do things that they want to do, and they are really protective of people that they care about, and from my point of view, he really cares about you," I replied.

As we piled into the car, we turned on the music and headed out toward the mall. I had googled it as soon as Miya said something about a mall, and we lucked out because the mall had just about everything we could think of. I could tell that this mall was for the saditty people because when we walked into the stores, everyone looked at us crazy. Luckily, I wasn't in the mood or else I would've shown my ass. But I had another plan for their ass. I had the salesperson help me with what I wanted, even if I didn't need it, and we headed to the checkout counter.

Once we got everything rung up, the cashier with her snobby ass told me the total. Without flinching, I pulled out my credit card and handed it to her.

"Ma'am, I'm going to need to see ID please," she replied.

Handing her my driver's license, I ran my credit card and started to bag up my items. As she was bagging up my items, I was slowly getting pissed.

"You know what, I don't want anything that I just purchased," I stated.

"Excuse me?" she replied.

"Yes, I would like to return everything that you just rang up," I said.

I didn't give a fuck that she had just rung up all the stuff that I wanted. I would take my business elsewhere. *The hell I look like?* The lady that was behind me, which was another black woman, looked at me and winked as she placed her things down and walked out of the store.

Once she finished refunding my card, I walked to the next store and purchased the exact same things that I had at the other but with a bunch of friendly ass people. As we all walked through the store making a purchase here and there, I wanted to take Justice into the Victoria's Secret store; she wasn't the girly type. I had been trying to encourage her to try new things because she was of age now. She was dating and living with a guy that cared about her, so it was time that she started to dress it up a little.

My little one-on-one trip with Justice turned into everyone coming along, and we just talked and tried on different things so that Justice would be comfortable with all of us to maybe do the same. Justice picked out a couple things that she liked, and she paid for them. She was starting to get comfortable with swiping her card and making purchases.

We stopped at the food court to get something to eat. We all sat around and tried to figure out what was the next store that we were going into. Justice wanted to see if she could find some shoes that would go with her prom dress. I didn't know what the dress was going to look like. She showed me the fabric that she was having the dressed made of, and it was so pretty. I knew that if we didn't find the shoes that Justice wanted, I would get in contact with Sade and have her look for some shoes that would go perfectly with her dress.

I was excited that Justice wanted to look for a couple things for prom since I didn't have any input in on her prom dress. We found all types of jewelry that she could wear. We weren't sure what would look better, so we grabbed a couple sets and would decide once we were able to go for a fitting. Justice said that she had a fitting in about two weeks, and I was going with her, come hell or high water.

As we grabbed out final things, we all loaded the bags into the car and headed back to the house. The moment that we walked into the house, all we could hear was yelling coming from the basement. We all headed that way to see what was wrong only to find all the men playing video games on all the televisions down there. I swear, it was like an arcade down there. It was loud as hell between the game and them yelling at each other.

We simply turned around and went back upstairs to put the things that we had bought in our rooms. My stomach was hurting me, but I thought that it had to do with the food that I ate in the mall. I sat down and scrolled through Facebook to locate the name of the funeral home that I wanted to call. I had seen some of their work, and it appeared that they were really good.

As I was waiting for someone to answer the phone, Kairo walked into the room and sat in the chair in the corner.

"Hello, my name is Asha, and I would like to make an appointment to come in and see about making arrangements for my mother," I said into the phone.

"Sure, ma'am. What day will be good for you?" the voice asked.

"Bae, when are we heading home?" I asked.

"We can head back tomorrow afternoon, so make it for the next day," he replied.

"Can I make the appointment for the day after tomorrow?" I asked.

"Let's see, I have an appointment at two and three. What time would work for you?' he asked.

"I'll do three o'clock," I replied.

"Okay, we have you set for three o'clock. We will see you then," he said and hung up.

"What's the matter, baby?" Kairo asked

"Nothing, my stomach feels a little funny," I replied.

"Go ahead and pack up when you are feeling better. Do you think that you are pregnant?" he asked with a grin.

"Boy, no. That is what you want, but no," I replied while turning over, looking out the window.

It felt like I had been sleeping for hours when I woke up. Looking at the clock, it had only been about thirty minutes. Going to the bathroom to relieve myself, I went to grab my clothes out of the laundry and started to pack my bags up. I didn't pack some of the stuff because I had plans on coming back in the near future for maybe a ladies' getaway, so my bags were light. When I made it downstairs, everyone was sitting around the house playing games and stuffing their faces of course.

"The fellas said that they would catch you on the next go-around," Kairo said, referring to Taj and them.

Sitting down next to him with a glass of water that I had gotten out of the kitchen, I watched as the men played spades and talked shit. Monica was surfing the internet trying to find a bag big enough to fix all her books and material in it.

"Girl, make sure you find me a bag too because I haven't even looked," I said.

"I can't believe that classes start in two weeks," Monica said.

"I know, right," I replied.

The whole time that I was talking to Monica, in the back of my head I was wondering if I could actually be pregnant. I was trying to think back if I had my cycle last month, to try to count the days, but I couldn't remember.

"Earth to Ash," Kairo said, standing in front of me.

The mere sight of him made me forgot about what I was thinking about, and I was now horny as ever.

"You really gonna sit there looking at that man like he is a whole snack?" Monica said.

"You damn right," I said, biting my lips.

Kairo bent down to me and kissed my lips, then whispered. "Keep looking like that, and we are gonna have to sneak off so I can dig in them guts," he said.

I swear, when he said that, I felt nothing but liquid flowing from between my legs; good thing that I was sitting on a towel, so no one could see. Robi came out of the house with a broom in her hands and started sweeping.

"Ro, put that damn broom down. I'll have the cleaning service coming in after we leave to get the house straight," Kairo said.

"Alright, baby," she replied.

The rest of the evening, we relaxed. We even ordered food in because Robi was finally tired of cooking. I had Kairo order me soup because my stomach still wasn't feeling all the way right. As the evening went on, I was scrolling through Facebook when I saw a post stating that Ameka had been missing and hadn't been seen for a couple days.

I was trying to figure out who this person was because it was a shared post, ND they even tagged her in the post.

Clicking on the tag, Ameka's page came up, and I scrolled through her pictures. It was a bunch of club pictures of course. I knew that Kairo said that she had children, but I didn't see one picture of them. She had pictures of her posted on Kairo's car, but none of him and her. In fact, he didn't have a Facebook, just an Instagram page, and I was all over that page.

We all got tired pretty early and decided that we would go to bed so we could get an early start and head home. When I laid down, my thoughts went back on to me possibly being pregnant. What if I was pregnant? I know Kairo would be happy, but what would that mean for me? I had hopes and dreams, and a baby wouldn't be something that I would want or need at the moment. I lay there thinking to myself as I drifted off to sleep.

KAIRO

As I woke up, I watched Asha as she slept quietly. She was so peaceful and angelic just lying there. My thoughts went to Asha and her recent stomachaches and began to wonder could she possibly be pregnant. Lord knows I had been wanting a child for a while, and this would be the motivation that I needed to slow it down in the game.

I walked down the hall to my office to find Mari sitting there, watching the news and cameras.

"Boy, y'all raised all kind of hell home. They still finding bodies and shit," Mari said.

"I had to let that nigga know who he was fucking with. Snake bastard didn't even show his face while his soldiers paid for his sins," I said.

"You ever find Ameka?" he asked.

I forgot to tell him about that slimy hoe. "Nigga, why she was fucking Nasir and his right-hand? We followed the right-hand, and he went straight to her house, and then he left and went to what I guess was his house after that. McCray calls me and tells me that she was fucking Nasir the whole time she was fucking with me," I replied.

"Yo, that's crazy," Mari responded.

As we were talking, Tez and Big came in the office. We closed the door because it would only be a matter of time before the ladies would wake up. I wanted to go ahead and get things in order before we made our way home. I had to get someone to watch the house that Tez was running since that fuck nigga wanted to run his mouth and go against the grain.

"So who are we going to put in that house?" I asked.

"What about the nigga Carlos on Blaze's crew? That nigga is loyal as fuck, and he's hungry," Mari said.

"Yeah, I think that need would work," Tez agreed.

"I'll talk with Blaze and see what she thinks. I can't be losing no money at all. That spot is a prime location," I replied

As we were talking, there was a news update that a body part was found floating in the river. I had to laugh because they would never be able to find all that nigga's parts. As we were talking, Blaze called me.

"What's up, B?" I asked.

"When y'all touch down?" she asked.

"Sometime tonight. I'm gonna hit you up when we do so you can come over," I replied.

Hanging up from her, I heard that the women were up and talking shit as usual. I swear, they talked shit more than the fellas and I did, and Robi's ass was the ringleader of course. There was a bang on the door and then Robi's voice.

"I know y'all rusty asses are in there. Bring y'all asses on and get these damn bags!" She fussed.

It couldn't get any better with her. I loved the fuck out of Robi and wouldn't know what to do if something was to happen to her. Opening the office door, we filed out, heading toward the living room where everyone was at.

"Robi, what you tryna get us to load up for, and you ain't even dressed?" I asked.

"Oh, I thought everyone was ready," she said.

Looking at all the ladies, they were trying to hold in their laugh, but Justice and Miya didn't last long.

"Y'all play too damn much," Mari said.

"Come on. Let's get dressed and load up so that we can stop and get something to eat," I said.

We all went our separate ways in the house so that we could pack up. It took Asha maybe thirty minutes to get herself together. She was dragging and pouting. I was assuming because she didn't want to go home and get back to reality. I took our bags down and loaded up my truck so Asha and I wouldn't be crammed in the van with the others. I told Robi to leave all those damn coolers in the garage because no one was loading them back into the van after she cursed me, Mari, Tez, and Big for laughing. She stomped away mumbling.

Locking the house up, we headed down the long road to the security booth. This was the first time that I had used the house, let alone needed any security. I was nervous about this company, but I had gotten them fully checked out before I hired them, and they gave me detailed reports daily on what was happening while I wasn't there. After I informed them that everyone was gone, he said that they would walk the grounds before they leave and send the final report.

As we headed to the nearest diner, Asha was saying

that her stomach was touching her back, and if she didn't eat soon, she was going to be sick. We walked into the diner and was seated quickly. The waitress walked over and took our drink orders as we looked over the menu. The whole time that everyone was looking at their menus, my eyes were on Asha. Her face was filling out, and I had noticed that her breasts were a little bigger also.

The waitress brought help to take all our orders because we were a large party. Once they finished taking our orders, I sat for a minute.

"Justice and Miya, what are your plans with school?" I asked.

"Well, we are both waiting to see if we get into Hopkins. If we don't, then UPenn it is," Miya replied.

"So y'all gonna do the dorm thing or an apartment?" I asked.

"I believe our freshmen year, we have to stay on campus, and after that, we can live off campus and have our cars," Justice replied.

"Well, Justice, Mari and I are going to take care of school, so don't worry about that. You're family now, and we take care of family," I stated.

When I said that, you should've seen the faces of Asha and Justice. I knew that Asha had been stressing trying to figure it out and poor Justice was just as worried.

Once the waitress brought our food, the table was quiet as hell. You could hear forks hitting the plates. The only people that were making sounds were Blessing and Paris, and that was because they were playing with toys. When we were finished, I paid the bill, and we all headed back to our trucks and cars to head home.

I turned on Pandora and headed home. I glanced over to Asha again, and she appeared deep in thought.

"What's the matter?" I asked, grabbing her leg.

"I'm just thinking about going to this funeral home to make these arrangements. I have to spread the word to people. I was thinking that it may be larger than I expected once I started telling people. I know she wasn't everyone's fan, but she did know a lot of people," she said.

"Look, we will handle the bill for the service and stuff. Just lay your mother to rest. Do y'all want us to come with y'all?" I asked.

"I think I need you to be there to get through this," she replied.

Hitting the button on the steering wheel, the radio started to ring.

"Yo," Mari said.

"Aye, we are going with Asha and Justice to make these arrangements," I stated.

"I'm cool with it. Wouldn't want it any other way," he replied.

Hanging up with Mari, it looked like a weight had been lifted off Asha's shoulders as she began scribbling down notes.

"What you are doing now?" I asked.

"I'm trying to figure out something nice to say about my mother to go in the obituary. Maybe I will let Justice do that," she replied.

We began talking about how things had gotten so bad between them, and Asha was still trying to figure it out herself. It was truly sad that they never got the chance to figure it out before it was too late. We made it home sooner than I expected to. When we pulled up to the house, there was a car parked at the front gate. It looked like it was a detective. Pulling up next to the car, I rolled the window down.

"Aye, yo! You are blocking my entrance," I stated.

"Mr. James?" the man asked.

"Yeah, that's me," I replied.

"Do you mind if I ask you a couple questions?" he asked.

I had never been scared to speak with the police, because anything that I tell them, they could verify, and that was a fact.

"Yeah, move out the way, and we can talk," I replied.

Pulling into the gate, he followed behind me. I parked my truck, and Asha and I jumped out and began to unload our bags and luggage.

"I'm Detective Rogers. Coming from a trip?" he asked.

"Yeah, little family vacay," I replied.

He followed us into the house, and I placed the bags down while Asha went to let the doors out the door.

"So what's up?" I asked.

"When was the last time you seen Ameka Brown?" he asked.

"It was a couple weeks back at my lady's job," I replied.

"So you haven't seen here since then?"

"No. Why do you ask?" I asked.

"Her family reported her missing a couple days ago, and her sister said that you and her were dating or had some type of relationship."

"Naw, we were not dating. It was nothing like that. We

hung out from time to time. You know, whenever I needed my dick wet," I said.

"Well, I got all the information that I need from you. Here is my card if you think of anything," he said, handing me his card.

As he pulled off, I threw his card in the trash. I didn't have a need for it. I carried our bags to the room so that once we finished running errands, we could unpack them. It was slightly after one, so I sat and watched TV for a little while. Asha sat on her laptop next to me.

We got up to get dressed to head to the funeral to make the arrangements for her mother. As we pulled up, Mari and Justice were pulling up at the same time. I watched Asha and Justice as they took deep breaths before entering the building.

"Hello, I'm Sasha. You must be Asha." The lady spoke.

"Yes, and this is my sister, Justice, my boyfriend, Kairo, and brother-in-law, Kamari," Asha stated.

"Hello. Sorry to be meeting in this sad case. Please, let's go into my office," she said.

"So my mother passed away last week, but we were out of town and couldn't make it back. She was in the house fire that was on the news a couple days ago," Asha stated.

"Oh gosh! So this will be a closed casket. Got it," Sasha said.

"My sister, Justice, is going to prepare the information for the obituary and get it over to you, along with pictures," Asha said.

"That's fine. Would you like to take a look at the caskets and make a selection? We will need to also select a burial place for her. I will need to get her clothes and undergarments no later than three days before the services," Sasha stated.

Looking over at Asha, she began to zone out again. She was taking this really hard, whether she wanted to admit it or not. We all had to keep snapping her out of it so that we could get through making this arrangement. We were finally finished and set the services for next Friday and Saturday. I knew a pastor that I had already asked to hold the service for Kandi. She wasn't a member of his church, but he knew her from going to school and once they got older. I was going to have Robi help Asha with getting things together for Kandi.

We all parted ways and headed home once we were finished. I had asked Asha if she wanted to stop and get something to eat, but she declined, saying that her stomach and head were hurting her again. Once we made it home, she went straight upstairs to lie down. I went into the living room and turned the TV to watch a movie. I went up a couple times to check on Asha and make her drink something, and I would come back down to finish watching TV.

I ended up falling asleep on the couch watching a movie. When I woke up, I turned the TV off, walked the house, and made sure that everything was locked and secured. When I walked into the room, Asha was still sleeping. I went into the bathroom to run me a shower. I went to turn on the bedroom light, and to my surprise, there was Asha lying in a pool of blood.

Running over to her side of the bed, I felt for a pulse, and it was barely there. I grabbed my phone and dialed 911.

"Help! I need help! There is blood everywhere!"

COMING 03/25!

CPSIA information can be obtained
at www.ICGtesting.com
Printed in the USA
LVHW111543270819
629113LV00005B/897/P

9 781091 482951